Snowy Strangeways

Melissa Tantaquidgeon Zobel

To Bonnie,
My dear neighbor &
a wonderful woman,

c/o
Melissa T. Zobel

UFP Fiction Series
Three Fires Confederacy Territory
Windsor, Ontario, Canada

Library and Archives Canada Cataloguing in Publication

Zobel, Melissa Tantaquidgeon, 1960-, author
      Snowy strangeways / Melissa Tantaquidgeon Zobel.

ISBN 978-1-988214-19-1 (softcover)

      I. Title.

PS3626.O24S66 2017   813'.6   C2017-907271-4

Book cover image: Emily Meyer
Book cover design: D.A. Lockhart
Book layout: D.A. Lockhart

The UFP Fiction Series is a line of books that showcases established and emerging voices from across North America. The books in this series represent what the editors at UFP believe to be some of the strongest voices in both American and Canadian fiction writing. *Snowy Strangeways* is the fourth book in this series.

Published in the United States of America and Canada by

 Urban Farmhouse Press
www.urbanfarmhousepress.com

Printed in Bell MT font

One day an army of gray-haired women may quietly take over the earth.
— Gloria Steinem

This book is dedicated to the Pequot people.

In 1637, English colonial captain John Mason engaged his Mohegan allies to join his soldiers in an attack on the Pequot village in what is now Mystic, Connecticut. Mason ordered his troops to set fire to Pequot wigwams, massacring women, children, and elders. In 1887, the Connecticut legislature passed a resolution to erect a statue in Mason's honor. In 1995, the Groton-Mystic town council agreed to remove that statue. The activists responsible for this removal included Eastern Pequots Lone Wolf Jackson and Ray Geer, as well as Mystic "Gray Goddesses" Melinda Plourde-Cole and Kate April. These champions of peace and justice inspired this work of fiction.

PART I
RETURN TO MYSTICK

CHAPTER 1
FAREWELL TO A GRAY GODDESS

"Witch!"

The word pierces my ears. Seaweed tea shoots out my nose. Through the three hundred-year-old window of the Silver Moon Café, I scan the banks of the river for the witch caller. Low-lying fog obscures all but the mast tops of the schooners, galleons, and whaling ships docked at Mystick, Connecticut's historic seaport. I cannot make out the tumbledown white colonial cottages that line the river. But their Gray Goddess owners are easy to spot. They crowd this café and every downtown street, wearing their signature wooden clogs, nubby handwoven tops, and organic granny skirts. None of them carries a cell phone or car keys or lives in a house that's less than two hundred years old.

Wait! I've spotted the witch-caller.

He's a weedy boy, shaking a finger at a Gray Goddess who is wading naked in the Mystick river. A hissing sound fills the air. It's coming from other Grays who have also discovered him. I find myself hissing along with them, automatically. The frightened boy darts down a narrow alley between the shop that sells whale oil lanterns and the one that peddles beeswax candles. He disappears, and a soothing hush falls over the café.

The Grays around me relax their arthritic shoulders and resume sipping seaweed tea at their wobbly colonial tables. A few of them blow grateful kisses at the portrait of Rebekah Wright that hangs over the soot-blackened central fireplace. The silver moons painted in her eyes give this establishment its name. Rebekah was the original owner of this building and Mystick's first Supreme Gray Goddess. Her husband called her a witch, slit her throat, and dumped her body into the Mystick

River.

A waitress about my age beelines for me, ignoring several tables that are vying for attention. She's rocking boy-band hair with a shock of gray, low-riding cargo shorts, and a khaki vest with a gazillion pockets. A scaffold piercing lays across one ear, and a beaded Native American earring dangles from the other.

"*That* was some serious shade that boy was throwing," she tells me, placing a platter on my table that's covered with miniature rose geranium scones in various geometric shapes. "Have one. It's on the house."

"Thanks," I say and select a crescent moon.

She drops into the seat beside me, in typically intrusive Gray fashion. "You're Snowy Strangeways, from New York. My condolences on the passing of your Grandma, Supreme Gray Goddess Slaney Strangways."

I slip down lower in my chair. "I thought changing my name and hair color would keep the locals from noticing me."

"Grays talk, sister." She grabs a scone from the platter and bumps it into mine, in some sort of foodie handshake. "I'm Lightning Brown, the Mohegan Tribe's youngest Gray Wolf."

"You're a Gray?" I motion to her un-gray clothing, hair, and jewelry, "You've got some lion tamer realness going on with your look, woman. How does a Gray get away with dressing like this, never mind cutting her hair so short?"

She snorts out a few scone crumbs, laughing. "Our Mohegan Gray Wolves don't share the Gray Goddesses' medieval wench dress code." Lightning points to my white-bleached razor-cut hair, heavily-shadowed crow black eyes, marigold leather miniskirt, and studded red stilettos. "Apparently, neither do you," she notes.

"Truth," I concur, scone bumping with her, a second time. "Why are you working at a musty old place like this?" I ask.

"Weekend job. Weekdays, I'm a security guard at Mohegan Sun on the rez in Uncasville. My grandma hooked me up with two summer jobs to keep me out of trouble. Come August, I'm back to studying architecture at Rhode Island School of Design." She stretches, and leans back, getting comfortable. "I hear you're also into design, like *your* grandma."

"Yes, I design interiors. No, my work is nothing like Slaney's. No knotted ship's rope, no dried starfish, no lumpy sea glass, no faded sailcloth upholstery." I raise an index finger. "Although," I grimace, "I did just inherit a house called Mermaid Cottage, with a cracked and peeling two hundred-year-old mermaid masthead business sign, out front."

Lightning snickers. Several Grays who failed to get served shoot her poisonous looks.

She cups a hand over my ear and whispers, "The Mystick Grays eat up that Shipwreck Chic. How'd you manage to take a different path?"

I hold up what's left of my crescent moon scone. "Slaney taught me how to create room layouts, right here with these scones." I push them around the platter. "One day when I was a kid, I placed a crescent shaped sofa around a hexagonal footstool." I grab more scones. "I stuck triangular chairs around a diamond-shaped dining room table. She realized that I was different. After my mom, Rebekah, was murdered, she sent me to The City to live with her A-list designer friend, Fríða Olafsdottir."

"Fríða? Impressive." She heaves a sigh. "I can't believe I forgot that your Mom was murdered."

"It's understandable. You were only a kid . . . like me," I breathe.

"Still, I'm really sorry about that. Wasn't she also an interior designer?"

"Yeah, but not for long. She died in her mid-twenties. Unlike her namesake, Rebekah Wright, the cops never figured out who slit Mom's throat."

"I thought the name Rebekah was taboo for all Grays?" wonders Lightning.

I nod at Rebekah's portrait. "It was and is. Slaney was a rebel. She named Mom to honor Mrs. Wright. She insisted that she was the last Mystick Gray to properly honor the Celtic goddesses— Cerridwen of the cauldron, Macha of the crow, and Arianrhod of the moon." I shake my head. "But shit, two murdered Gray Rebekahs? Sometimes taboos are taboo for a reason."

"I hear you. The way I heard Rebekah Wright's story, she started the Gray Goddesses after her husband, Cyrus, and his English bros burned down the Pequot village on this river in 1637. Pequot women got proactive and formed the Gray Foxes. My Mohegan ancestors—who had allied with the English in that battle—created the Gray Wolves. These women's societies met to forge a peace. But once Cyrus found out his wife was conspiring with the Natives, he accused her of the big W, and . . ." She motions across her throat, "that was it."

"Yup. Didn't his portrait used to hang somewhere in this restaurant?" Snowy scopes the room.

"Good memory. It used to hang upside down." Lightning rolls her tongue in her cheek and points to the little-used men's room. "I took it upon myself to relocate it to the floor behind the urinal."

"Nice touch." I raise my mug full of seaweed tea. "You're giving me life."

A Gray with a thick Boston accent calls Lightning's name from the kitchen.

She puts her hands on my shoulders. "Grays support Grays. You're going to be an amazing Gray, one day. Gimme a call when your hair turns, Strangeways."

I snort. "Sure, in like thirty years?"

"Or thirty minutes," clucks Lightning, looking back over her shoulder. "There are more young Grays appearing, every day. Mother Earth is in trouble. She can't wait until we all wrinkle, to help out."

Warning bells clang, signaling the opening of this town's steampunk drawbridge and the start of Slaney's burial at sea. The Grays around me rise. I drop a ten on the table and follow their lead.

Lightning calls to me, as I pass the register, "May your grandma have a good journey to the other side." She pats her heart. "Come visit me at Mohegan. I'll be waiting for you."

"Thanks for the wishes." I salute her. "But once this Gray funeral hocus pocus is over, I'm grabbing my suitcase from Mermaid Cottage and hopping the next train back home to New York City."

I follow the Grays out onto the misty river that's filling up with handcrafted wooden vessels. A drum roll sounds and all eyes turn to the still-covered barge. A pillar straight Gray Goddess dressed in white flax yanks a pulley to lift the tarp that's covering the funeral vessel. Every Gray head in the crowd shoots back, stunned, at first sight of this newly appointed funeral barge that shimmers in a glossy navy blue. The name "Slaney" gleams in metallic gold on the hull. The "S" resembles a swimming mermaid. A white silk sailcloth canopy painted with a glittering silver moon hangs from shiny brass poles at the four corners of the casket. Each pole is topped with fluffy white ostrich feathers. It's spectacular in a typically Gray kind of way. The décor reminds me of something I once saw in a British history book.

But where is the captain?

Who is the captain?

No one but Slaney's lawyer knows the identity of the person honored with commanding the barge that will carry her oak coffin down the river and into the Atlantic sea. A shrill boatswain's whistle sounds, letting us know it's time for Slaney's barge to set sail. A wiry old man with a steel wool beard and a scarred left eyelid discreetly dashes on board. Spectators lean in for a better look. One Gray starts gagging when she identifies him. Dozens of liver spotted fists begin to shake in his direction. Hissing noises, once again, fill the air. For Grandma Slaney's barge captain is none other than the notorious Riley Finch.

The crowd shouts predictable questions—

"Wasn't he accused of kidnapping that little girl?"

"Is this Slaney's way of forgiving him and restoring his reputation?"

"Yes and no," I mumble to myself.

Slaney never forgave Riley for kidnapping Amani Jones. She merely chose the most qualified person to construct and design her barge. Our historic Mystick Seaport is home to the world's top wooden boat wrights, and Riley Finch is the best of their lot. He even looks fairly respectable, in his well-pressed Navy dress coat. If only he'd done a better job trimming his beard. The Gray who was gagging at first sight of him removes her sunglasses, and I could swear it's Alse Critchley, the Supreme Gray Goddess who preceded Slaney. But of course, this can't be Alse because she fled town eight years ago as a wanted fugitive, after poking out Riley's right eye for the kidnapping.

The boat loving mourners begin to gush over Riley's craftsmanship:

"He must have used ten coats of paint from Holland to get that sheen on the hull."

"The tight cedar planking had to be shipped in from Prince of

Wales Island."

"Those enormous ostrich feathers must have come from that special farm in South Africa."

I count to ten, waiting for the predictable shift in public opinion. Sure enough, I hear—

"That Amani Jones girl was retrieved unharmed from Riley's place. Wasn't she?"

"Maybe it was all a big misunderstanding about the kidnapping."

"The court found him innocent, after all."

"What if he was protecting the child from someone or something?"

"Ole Riley did a great job with that barge. He's not such a bad guy."

A second shrill whistle indicates that Slaney's funeral barge is nearing the end of the river and about to enter the sea.

Fake Alse opens her arms to the crowd and then pulls them back, as if collecting energy. With each motion, her wrinkled cheeks seem to smooth, her rounded back straightens, and her North Atlantic gray eyes brighten to a blinding Brazilian parrot blue. Like the legendary Succubus, she draws in the energy of this gathering. People around me nod at one another, affirming that this eccentric stranger must indeed be the real Alse Critchley, somehow rejuvenated by the powerful energy of this funeral.

Each time the ship slaps the crest of a frothy wave, Riley's sagging right eyelid flutters open, exposing the motionless glass eyeball that replaced the real one taken out by the tip of Alse Critchley's cane. The sun has burned off the morning fog, and the now-sparkling water helps me remember that Riley once told me my sparkling crow-colored eyes could "catch anything, be it fish, fowl, angel, or devil." I still cling to this superstition. One day, I'd love to catch the devil that murdered my mom.

Another drum roll sounds. A theatrical spotlight flashes on. It follows my eight-year-old cousin, Moira O'Connor, as she steps up to the Gray podium by the drawbridge. She's doing our grandma proud, wearing an unbleached muslin dress and a seagrass wreath on her boiled lobster hair that brings out the pale green of her eyes. Her best friend, Nahla Prakesh, is standing on the riverbank in a soccer uniform and cleats. Nahla pulls her eggplant-colored hair into a ponytail, highlighting her perfect diamond-shaped face and shining olive eyes.

She cheers on her friend, "You're dope, Moira!"

Moira blushes but quickly lifts a glowing whale oil lantern over her head, and bellows with unnatural authority for a third grader, "I will keen for my grandmother."

Keen?

I haven't heard this term used since right after Mom died, when Slaney declared, "There will be no keening for Rebekah." This riled me, even though I was only a kid. Keening is how the Irish honor the dead in song, and my family prides itself on its Irish heritage.

Moira opens her mouth and lets loose a bell-like sound that calms the wild river whitecaps into a gentler roll. Every Gray in this crowd watches, rapt; they know she will lead them one day. Moira's very name means "fate" or "destiny." Her enchanting singing also guarantees that no one notices the splash of Slaney's heavy oak coffin as it falls into the sea. Well, almost no one. I feel a thunderbolt strike my gut the moment it happens. I know Moira feels it, too, because her singing falls flat on her final notes.

My Aunt Selkie—Moira's mom—is glaring at me instead of watching her kid keen. She's angry that Slaney did not leave her the family decorating business in her will. I try to ignore her by focusing on our fine local bagpiper, Murray Finney, now stepping forward to play the "Cliffs of Dooneen." His music always concludes these sorts of public Gray rituals. A salty tear falls onto my lip when he reaches the line, *You may travel far far from your own native home. Far away oer the mountains far away oer the foam.*

"Farewell, Grandma Slaney," I whisper to the roiling river that flows to the sea.

I wipe my damp eyes, taking care not to dislodge my false eyelashes or smudge my heavy silver eyeshadow. The Grays all raise their arms to the moon. I lift mine and close my eyes. Together, we bid farewell to Mystick's Supreme Gray Goddess, Slaney Strangeways, now returned to her eternal resting place in the Great Salt Sea.

CHAPTER 2
PERHAPS FRIEND

With eyes closed, I picture my grandmother as she appears in the self-portrait that hangs in her stark white living room— a suntanned sinewy woman with knobby wrinkled knees, sitting on an oak barrel in a short white cotton nightgown, trapped inside an underwater room made of glass. Her lanky toes and fingers stretch in front of her, expressing a desire to reach through that glass to touch the flora and fauna of the surrounding seascape. A golden beeswax candle with a lighted flame pokes recklessly out of her nightgown pocket, though she seems not to notice, for her head is tossed back in a radiant silver blur, as if her hair is made of moonbeams.

This is how I will always remember her.

I startle when a familiar voice calls, "Snowy?"

A short, pudding-shaped Gray in an outdated spirit blue suit puts a hand on my arm. It's my godmother, Supreme Gray Wolf Gertie Mazeen, from the Mohegan Indian Reservation. The remaining ungray strands left in her hair nearly match my natural toad brown color. My dark eyes match hers, as well. Most Gray Goddess offspring are clones of Slaney—leggy women, with hair, eyes, and skin like sun, sea, and sand. I only got the height and endless legs.

I pat the protective wampum feather necklace Gertie gave me, to let her know I'm still wearing it under my shirt.

Gertie also pats the hidden necklace. "Good to see you're wearing protection." She folds her arms over her stomach, perturbed. "I suppose you're already heading back to The City."

"On the next train," I confirm.

Her more fashionable friend, Supreme Gray Fox Edith Wyouggs from the Pequot Reservation steps into our conversation.

"That sounds like an excellent idea," concurs Edith. Her blunt-cut silver hair, fitted black linen dress, erect posture, sharp heels, porcupine quill earrings, and judgmental eyes make me stand up straighter. After what the Mystick colonists did to Edith's people back in 1637, she has good cause to maintain a razor's edge when she visits this town. Gertie pokes her discourteous friend.

"I'm only thinking of the girl's safety, Gert," demurs Edith. "Her family is prone to trouble, and the youngsters in our tribes have been up to far too much mischief, lately. Snowy needs to steer clear of them."

"What sort of mischief?" I ask.

"Dabbling in medicine that's too big for their britches," snaps Gertie. "You're an urbane young woman, Snowy. But sometimes the reservation can be far more dangerous than the city."

"I hear you!" I say. "This quaint little town is the most dangerous place I know. Slaney ran it, yet even she couldn't find out who killed her own kid."

Edith's lovely upturned eyes narrow. "That was a terrible business, Snowy. You were so young. Do you remember any of the events leading up to your mom's death?"

"I recollect one incident in particular. The day before she died, Mom was trying out a bold new color palette for the house next door. Slaney hated it and accused Mom of suffering from The Gray Curse. Mom claimed Slaney suffered from 'a banal sense of color.' Slaney took off for The City and Mom headed for The Banshee Pub." I grit my teeth and shudder. "Why are we talking about this, again?"

"Because, my dear," explains Edith, "I've suggested the Grays reopen the investigation into your mom's death,"

I eye Edith, curiously. "*You've* suggested they reopen Mom's case. You hated her. I've often wondered if you weren't the one who killed her."

"Snowy!" exclaims Gertie.

Edith pats Gert's arm with a well-manicured hand. "No, that's fair," she concludes. "It's true that I never liked Rebekah. Nobody did.

But I still want her murder solved because violent people must be punished for their misdeeds."

"We can agree on that," I reply.

"What happened at Mermaid Cottage on the day of the murder?" asks Edith, leaning in.

My eyes glaze over. "The place was quiet when I got home, except for the soft hum of the refrigerator and a light dripping sound, like a leaky faucet. My growling stomach prompted me to dash straight to the freezer in search of a microwavable mac and cheese. But Barnacle Bill blocked my entrance to the kitchen.

"Barnacle Bill?" scoffs Edith.

"Slaney's cat," explains Gertie. "Riley Finch is now caring for him."

"Which is another weird topic," I say. "Anyway, the day mom died, I reached out to snatch his raggedy black tail, and he dodged to one side. I caught the end of his back leg and he craned his neck around and sunk his teeth into my palm. A few drops of my blood spilled on the floor. I swatted him and he slinked away, whimpering. That's when I noticed the dripping sound had stopped. I stepped into the kitchen and froze. Mom's body lay sprawled on the floor in a crimson pool of blood. Her clogs lay beside her, upside down, like the time Gertie turned over my sneakers for good luck. There were also words written in blood on her upper chest."

"Did you tell the police *all* that?" asks Edith.

"Many times. But they'd already decided I was some sort of psycho-killer-kid. They asked me whether I hated Mom's numerous boyfriends, resented her heavy workload, or enjoyed playing with knives. Then they moved on to the truly wacked questions like, 'Who picked that bright shade of green paint in the kitchen she was working on, next door?'"

I hear someone cackling and discover it's Alse. Her disdainful laughter is aimed at a guy holding a retro copper pen and flip notepad. His eyes are honey brown and his skin is the color of a wet beach. His sandy ringlets remind me of twisted driftwood. He catches me checking him out. Edith and Gertie—still talking beside me—are completely forgotten. A soft smile flashes across his face, accentuating the deep horizontal scar across the middle of his nose. I tell myself to overlook his rumpled shirt. I recognize him as a local reporter named Kai Corby. Slaney mailed me his article praising the Grays for biking to work and shunning digital technology. At the time, I was considering buying my first cell phone, and his article talked me out of it. That sort of Gray propaganda is typical of *Mystick Lights* newspaper, which used to be owned by Alse, and—come to think of it—probably still is.

I bid my Gray ladies goodbye just as Kai disappears behind the new fog bank that's rolling in like the ghosts of Gray Goddesses' past. I recall how I used to love racing this Mystick River fog across the draw-bridge, as a kid. Just as this thought crosses my mind, Moira runs across the slick steel bridge gratings. Her foot slips, hurtling her towards the low end of the railing. Her lobster hair flashes like a flame about to be extinguished. I don't budge, even though it looks like she'll tumble into the river. Kai lunges and grabs her, just in time.

Shame burns on my cheeks. Why did I freeze? Is it because all kids are like aliens to me? Or am I merely jealous of Moira? I know Slaney would have left everything to her, if the kid were old enough. Moira was her favorite because she loves the river, the sea, and all things Gray. At least I appreciate the shoreline and interior design, like Slaney. My Aunt Selkie hates the water, which is pretty funny considering she was named after a mystical sea creature. She and Rebekah were half-sisters. The identity of Rebekah's dad remains a total mystery. At least there'a story attached to Selkie's paternity. Local gossip claims Selkie was the biological byproduct of a brief affair between Slaney and a desert Bedouin during her gap year in the Middle East. But Moira doesn't take after her mom's side at all. She's a combination of her Grandma Slaney and her handsome Irish freight train of a dad, Clancy O'Connor, who is probably watching his daughter from the window of the Banshee Pub with some new side chick.

Kai walks Moira back to Selkie, who missed her daughter's near-brush with disaster. I don't think anyone except Kai and me caught this scene, until I hear someone clapping and realize its Alse Critchley.

"Perhaps I judged you too harshly, Mr. Corby," she says, curling the corners of her thin mouth into a knowing grin.

"You're giving me a second chance?" he gasps.

Alse blinks in an exaggerated way.

"Great," says Kai, pressing his monogrammed copper pen into the permanent notch in his middle finger, poised for a scoop. "I'll bet you've never seen anything like this funeral, before."

Alse shakes her beak of a nose at him, like it's a scolding finger. "I most certainly have seen the like! This event reminds me of Lord Nelson's funeral." She punches a knuckle at the rough river. "I can still see his lavish barge now, with its fluffy black ostrich feathers and impeccable gold paint, sailing down the Thames." She winks at Kai. "There are similarities between Slaney's sendoff and old Horatio's funeral, to be sure. What a fine time we Grays had that day in foggy London town!"

I snap my fingers, in recognition. That's it! Slaney's barge reminds me of the painting of Lord Nelson's funeral barge. Kai's head flops to his chest when he also makes the connection and realizes that Lord Nelson died two centuries ago. Alse is taunting him; Pressing her hand to her heart, she tosses back her mane and cackles like a mean teenager. Her pose reminds me of a photographic negative of Slaney's self-portrait. Both images show beautiful long gray haired women expressing head-tossed ecstasy. Only Alse draws mean-spiritedness inward like a black hole, while Slaney radiates healing white light like a newborn star.

Kai shuffles my way, muttering, "This assignment blows." He sticks his notepad under his armpit and his pen atop his ear.

I shove a hand under his downcast face. My nails feature swirling details from Van Gogh's 'Starry Night.'

He shakes it, staring at my nails. "I'm Kai Cor-by," he stutters.

"Snowy Strangeways," I say, as our hands join with a shock of electricity.

"Wow!" We echo.

I point to his pen and the paper he's using to take notes. "You're serving some serious retro," I note.

"Retro?" His honey-colored eyes lock onto mine. "Should I be insulted?"

"That depends. Do you work on a roll top desk with a banker's lamp?"

"Actually, I do, Snowy," he chuckles. "Love your name by the way."

I catch him checking out my legs, which is typical.

I lift his chin. "I picked it because birth names suck," I explain. "Most people want to change theirs but don't do it for fear of pissing off their parents. Lucky for me, I don't have any parents to piss off. Fríða Olafsdottir became my guardian eight years ago. Her busy schedule meant I was raised by the women at Hips, the exotic dance club next door. They showered me with hot hand-me-downs, taught me how to apply artful makeup, and nurtured me, something Fríða was incapable of doing."

"You were raised by strippers? That's pretty hot." He furrows his delicious eyebrows. "I'm also an orphan. My dad's dead and my mom ditched me."

I swat the air. "You're my mirror image! My mom's dead and my dad ditched me." I slide a hand onto a projected hip, channeling my nannies' charm. "I've seen your photo and byline in *Mystick Lights* newspaper. Kai is a sickening name by the way."

"Sickening in a good way, right?" Kai surveys my clothes and makeup like I'm some bizarre bird from a far-off galaxy.

I give him two thumbs up.

"I didn't pick it, myself," he says. "It isn't the one I was born with, either. My adoptive mom gave it to me."

My eyes widen, pulling him in deeper. "Is she a Gray?"

"Most definitely," he snorts.

I hold one hand to my heart and the other backwards on my forehead. "Is Kai a typical Gray Goddess name? I mean, does it tie you to the water, and therefore your Mom?"

He ticks off three fingers, "It means 'ocean' in Hawaiian, 'pier' in Estonian, and 'safe harbor' in German."

"I'm feeling that." I lower my false eyelashes. "As a Gray child, you must select at least one of those watery identities." I clutch both hands to my heart. "So you can spiritually claim it." I stick out my tongue and cross my eyes.

He holds his stomach, chuckling. "You're killing me. How old are you, anyway?"

"Eighteen, give or take."

"Give or take what?"

"My mood. And you?"

"Twenty-two, regardless of my mood." He strokes his chin. "You seem to know a lot about the Grays, and I notice you picked a water name for yourself."

I groan, realizing I shouldn't have implied so much Gray knowledge. "You could say the name Snowy relates to water. But that's not why I picked it. I chose it when I bleached my hair white. Unlike the all-natural Gray ladies, I enjoy being a creature of my own design."

He moves in. "I'd like you to consider some of Kai's non-watery meanings. In Finnish, it means 'perhaps,' and in Tagalog it means 'friend.'"

"All right then, 'Perhaps Friend' Kai, let me ask you something." I squint, probingly. "Aren't you a bit young for a newspaper reporter?"

"Nelly Bly was already a famous journalist at eighteen." He puffs up a bit. "I've already graduated from Connecticut College. Where do you go to school?"

"Already graduated from Parsons, in The City," I cough.

"At eighteen?" He steps backwards. "How is that even possible?"

"I'm almost nineteen if it makes you feel any better. I work for Fríða as an interior designer at Víðsýni Studio in Manhattan."

"Víðsýni?"

"In her Icelandic language, it means 'an expansive, open-minded view of the world.'"

"Good name." He nods. "I can't believe you're only eighteen and already a licensed interior designer, like Slaney Strangeways."

I bite my lip. "Correction. Underage, *un*licensed, and nothing like Slaney. She lived in a quaint colonial cottage and designed rooms in a barn stained in Little Mermaid shades of seafoam, mussel shell, and aquamarine. I work in an asymmetrical, putty-colored, glass and steel industrial warehouse in The City."

I crane my neck to stare out to sea, hoping to catch a final glimpse of Slaney's barge. But I can no longer spot it. I wander toward the river's edge. My toes teeter over a rocky crag. Kai grabs my hand and yanks me backwards.

"Careful," he cautions, gently.

"Thanks," I whisper, reconnecting with the living, through the warmth of his hand.

I wish that hand did not feel so good. My sudden fascination with this guy is bad, bad, bad. I suffer bizarre visions when I get too curious about anyone or anything. The shrinks tell me it's due to my post-traumatic stress caused by stumbling upon Mom's murder scene as a kid. My freaky visions always begin with geometric shapes that morph into home furnishings and room décor. This weird talent has cost me a few relationships: like the time I told a guy I liked that his new mustard-colored sofa didn't complement his wallpaper before he'd invited me inside his apartment. He thought I was either a bitch, a witch, or a psycho. As a member of a family of Grays, some might say I'm all three.

Kai is none of the above. His rumpled but expensive shirt tells me he lives with a busy mom who buys him stuff but won't do his laundry. The dent in his middle finger comes from overusing his monogrammed copper pen, which was surely a high school graduation gift. His penetrating eyes suggest that he maintains an obsessive hobby.

Sports cars? No, that's too pricey, even for a rich kid his age.

Baseball collectibles? Far too cliché.

Surfing? Too left coast.

I'd guess sailing—as that's the default hobby in this town—but his eyes appear too book-worn for any outdoor passion.

The most obvious choice is the correct one: his newspaper work and hobby are somehow related.

I catch Alse bidding farewell to a ponytailed Gray who looks like she's from the Upper West Side. She reminds me of someone famous. But her floppy hat and sunglasses make it impossible to get a good look at her face. When they separate, Alse strides toward *Mystick Lights* newspaper office.

"Please don't tell me Alse Critchley lives in my office building," Kai shrinks.

"The truth can be tough," I tisk. "You should have been more careful about what you said to her. She's the best person to explain the Grays' history and symbolism to you, never mind the fact that she obviously signs your paycheck."

Kai doesn't hear that last jab. "What the . . .?" he gasps.

He's pointing to a spot on the river where several more Grays have stripped off their clothes and begun swimming, like hoary mermaids. I flush with embarrassment until I see the transcendent expressions on their faces. I consider explaining to Kai that they've entered the spiritual space that Gertie calls "the shades of gray." But I stop myself, in time.

Kai prods, "You must have some idea what's going on with all the buff bathing."

I feel the urge to whisper, "Witches," in a spooky voice. But I can't do that with so many of the old bats within earshot. Besides, why bother cupcaking? I'm a short-timer in this town.

I smooth my white hair and answer, "No clue. As noted, I'm not a member of the Gray sisterhood and never intend to be."

Kai brushes the jagged ends of my hair with the back of his hand. "I'm glad you've dodged Gray style. I don't get these women. Even the ones our age dress like feudal peasants. Their favorite downtown shops carry beeswax candles and whale oil lanterns. Whale oil! Seriously! Where do they even get whale oil? They act as if the automobile has yet to be invented, never mind the cell phone." He removes a cheesy burner phone from his pocket and shakes it at me. "I may be retro but I don't completely shun technology, like these crazy old crones."

Several Grays flash their bicycle lights as they ride past us, indicating strong disapproval of his remarks. It's clear that Kai's support of the Gray lifestyle in his old article was due to some editor's arm-twisting.

"Kai, I can't believe you're throwing public shade on the leading ladies of Mystick," I pan.

One side of his mouth raises, creating a dimple in his tan cheek. "I doubt you're much different, Snowy. I'm surprised to find someone with your "Víðsýni" attending this quaint small-town funeral." He smirks and raises an eyebrow. "Were you close to the late Slaney Strangeways?"

"We're related," I say in a hushed tone.

His head flies back. "I'm so sorry. My condolences. I didn't know Slaney had any living family left, other than her daughter Selkie, her granddaughter Moira, and that little girl who left town after . . ." His eyes widen and he straightens up, instantly more professional. "Would you care to offer a quote for the paper to memorialize Ms. Strangeways' passing?"

"Sure." I open my arms, as if delivering a church eulogy. "Slaney was like a ray of sunlight shining through water - bright, lovely, and slightly bent." I cock my head to one side.

"Interesting epitaph." Kai scribbles in a form of shorthand I thought died out with hieroglyphics.

I drum on his notepad. "Please be sure to cite me as a family member who would rather not be."

He sinks a little. "I'm just the opposite. I'd love to know anything about my birth family. I have but a single clue to my biological mom's identity."

I flash eager jazz hands. "Spill!"

He grimaces. "When I was a kid, my Mom said that if I wasn't a good boy, I'd be condemned to live incognito, like my birth Mother."

"Incognito? Fascinating. What is Gray Mama hiding about Birth Mama?"

"Well, rumor has it . . ."

His words are cut off by a squeal, coming from the naked shivering Grays, who are nudging one another out of the river. Despite the fact that it's July, a chilly wind is blowing in from the ocean.

Kai squints. "You really have no clue about the significance of the nude bathing?"

I sneer in the bathers' direction. "Like I said: not my sideshow."

He scratches his head. "You're different from other Mystick women. I don't suppose you'd consider delaying your return to The City to take on a local design job."

I tilt my head and bat my lashes, fawn-like. "Seriously?"

"I mean it," he says, "my mom has been looking for a designer to redo the interiors of our house."

I envision a white shoreline cottage, ungapatched with old buoys, lobster pots, and wreaths made of scallop shells. A wave of nausea comes over me.

"Sorry, my Perhaps Friend," I rebuff. "Your mom would hate my work. I slay geometric shapes with urban mojo. You won't find a single sailboat or anchor in my interiors."

"Perfect!" delights Kai. "She hates Gray style. My mom is icy and cosmopolitan, not the nurturing type." He grins. "I know you'll get along."

I plant my hands on my hips. "Hey!"

"That wasn't meant to be offensive." Kai shuffles through his art deco wallet and hands me a business card with words that glitter in a lavender font.

Lyr Corby, Ombudswoman
Granite House
1-555-GRANITE

I tuck the card under my lacy pink bra strap. "Granite House? Not your typical Gray homestead. Some people say it once served as an institution for lunatic Grays."

"That must have been before they bought their rehab center in Brazil for members who suffer from The Gray Curse." He leans in and whispers, "Between you and me, I think 'cursed' is their old-fashioned code word for depression, bipolar disorder, schizophrenia or any mental health condition."

I picture Mom's argument with Slaney the day before she died and speak without thinking. "I think it has something to do with artistic overdrive." He scrutinizes me, and I swat my hand, dismissively. "But what do I know? I'm the Anti-Gray."

"In a way, so is my mom." Kai eyes the business card sticking out of my bra strap. "You should visit Granite House and meet Lyr."

"I'll admit that I'm curious," I muse.

As soon as that last word leaves my lips, a spiral flashes before my eyes, followed by circles and rectangles. This is how my visions always begin. First come the shapes, followed by the furniture. I expect to see the inside of Granite House. But I get nothing. I heave a sigh, grateful not to fall into a vision, right now, because visions can make me lose touch with reality, even black out and forget things.

I force myself to resume our discussion. "What does an ombudswoman do, exactly?" I ask. "I know corporations and governments hire them to handle disputes. But no one seems to know much about them.

The biggest companies around here are the Mohegan and Pequot casinos. I'm guessing Lyr works for one of those tribes."

He doesn't respond. I bump him with my hip, to provoke an answer. "Is that right?"

"Something like that," he swallows.

"Oh, hell on hot rollers!" I exclaim, catching the time on the church tower clock..

He mouths my words, eyes bulging.

"Sorry Kai, I still need to grab my suitcase from Mermaid Cottage before I can catch the train to Manhattan. It was nice meeting you, Perhaps Friend Kai."

I dash down Main Street, in the direction of River Road. Shapes begin to fill my head, transforming into the interior of a room with a roll top desk and banker's lamp, surrounded by antique newspaper memorabilia and a fluffy white king-sized bed. My eyesight blurs, and I slow down.

Kai calls out from behind, "I hope to see you again, slippery snow woman."

I feel a warm flush and am about to conjure a pithy comeback, when I spot Fríða. I should have known she'd show up. She's arguing with a tiny gem of a woman with hair that is dyed plum and shaved short on one side, and cut chin length and dyed lavender on the other. Fifth Avenue labels drip off her size two frame. The girls at Hips would love her serious Gotham style. The only thing about her that reeks of Mystick is the heavy purple quahog and natural pearl pendant weighing down her narrow neck.

I'm not surprised to see Fríða quarreling. Despite the smaller woman's chic appearance, Fríða always complained about the Mystick Grays' dumbass small town views. Her mind is as broad as the North Atlantic, which makes it difficult for me to live up to her standards. That's why, when I designed Víðsýni's showroom this Spring, I put my best geometric spin on the space— installing a circular Italian sofa, satellited by a half moon ottoman, two triangular end tables, and several teardrop chairs, all in primary colors like an updated Alexander Calder mobile. Clients loved it. So did Fríða. I was glad not to disappoint because she gave up a lot to raise me and teach me her interior design trade.

Fríða adjusts her wig, checks her wristwatch, and bolts for the train station in lethal heels that would be absurd for someone half her age. I glance at the white clock tower of the Mystick Church. Shoot! It's nearly noon. I can't make it back to Mermaid Cottage and still catch the train. But I might be able to catch Fríða. I pick up the pace and shout her name. She doesn't hear me. I push myself, running so fast that my chest burns. She's in crazy good shape for an old woman. I am almost within earshot when a wet, naked Gray collapses right in front of me. A web of iron hair covers her motionless face. I freeze for a second, debating what to do, then I remember how I dropped the ball on rescuing Moira. I drop to my knees and scoop her head off the ground to see if she's breathing. She's not. I hail a police officer for help.

In the distance, a man yells something that sounds like doo-was yoo-mas. Those strange words make my skin crawl. I scan to see where his voice is coming from. I spot him, a skinny guy on the roof of the Silver Moon Café. He's carrying a leather binder and wearing a long charcoal gray coat, like somebody from one of those late twentieth century vampire television shows.

I'm flustered by the strange familiarity of his words and the fact that the woman in my arms still doesn't appear to be breathing. A paramedic pushes me aside and works to resuscitate her. I stumble backwards and watch the desperate life-saving process. *Still no breathing.* I re-scan for the man in the gray coat and notice my train pulling out of the Mystick station.

The words of the man on the roof echo inside my brain. Doo-was yoo-mas. They feel important. But I can't place them. Adrenaline surges through me. I squeeze my pounding head. The words thunder between my ears. I roll them around in my mind, considering them.

Two more paramedics push past me. I close my eyes and try to send the dying woman some healing energy, like Gertie used to do when I was sick as a kid.

Nothing.

Doo-was yoo-mas. Doo-was yoo-mas. Doo-was yoo-mas.

My focus remains on these words that are somehow familiar and important. But I still can't place them. The throbbing inside my skull becomes unbearable.

The fallen woman gasps in an enormous breath. I feel myself

gasp, as well. I didn't realize I'd been holding my breath during her struggle.

Geometric shapes burst into my mind. I expect them to transform into furniture from the interiors of the fallen woman or the yelling man. But they turn into lines, then letters, then words. Blurry words. I struggle to focus and can finally read them. They say: "Do as you must."

That's what the guy on the roof was saying! Doo-was yoo-mas! Do as you must! I can't believe it. This is the same phrase I found written in blood on my dead mom's chest.

CHAPTER 3
RATSNAKE GRAY

I push through the fake colonial double doors of the Mystick Police Station. To my child's eyes, this building was a shadowy bat and spider-infested dungeon, filled with demon torturers. Now all I see is a tacky bureaucratic shitbox. Blinding fluorescent lights reveal ripped vinyl seats, water-stained drop ceilings, and cracked vinyl floors.

Two women cops—a rookie and an old-timer—are slugging beige Dunkin Donuts coffee, behind a cheap laminate reception desk.

The older cop with the frizzy gray ponytail takes a bite out of her maple donut. "How much do you think that fancy funeral barge cost?" she asks.

The swaggery younger cop with short-cropped hair sneers. "Those Grays don't care. They're all rich trust fund broads. They only pretend to make their living as artists."

The older cop drops her donut. "You shouldn't talk about the Grays like that."

I recognize the rookie and snap my fingers, "Hey, I know you. We attended Mystick Elementary School together. You stayed back the same year that I skipped first grade, which is how we wound up in Mrs. Cunningham's second grade class, together." I tap a finger on my well-glossed lips. "In fact, you once called my mom a pasta-toot. So, I nick-named you Hairy Turd."

The rookie spits out her coffee and huffs, "The name is Officer Mary Burd!"

"What do you want, Strangeways?" she grinds.

"I have new information about my mom's murder case."

"It's a cold case. I can't see the hurry," her older colleague inserts.

"Maybe that's why so many of your cases stay cold," I huff.

"Hey, watch it, kid!" the older cop booms, wiping her hands on a napkin. "Looks like you hoofed it here all the way from your grandma's funeral. Didn't you pull the same stunt on the day of your mom's murder?" She leers. "If memory serves, you refused a ride home from school and stupidly decided to walk down River Road, alone, with a kidnapper on the loose."

"My mom was busy working on the interiors of Monster House . They had no utilities yet."

"Monster what?"

"Monster House. That's my nickname for the rambling, stormy gray Victorian, right next door to Mermaid Cottage."

"Figures. What was your Grandma Slaney's excuse for not picking you up?" the older cop asks.

"She was out of town, visiting her friend Fríða in the city."

"You couldn't wait for an adult to give you a lift, like a normal kid?" injects Mary.

"No, I opted out of a charity ride from some teacher or parent that was already luney tunes over the recent child kidnappings, which your department never solved. You probably don't remember, HT, but Amani was the second local girl to go missing; Lucy Wauby from the Pequot Reservation was the first. Plus, I wasn't worried about Riley Finch stuffing me into a shed, like he did to Amani. He was Slaney's boyfriend and a family friend."

"Your family keeps interesting company," observes Mary.

"Enough waltzing down memory lane," grumbles the older cop. "What's your new news?"

"A man at Slaney's funeral shouted the words I found written in blood on my dead mom's chest," I snarl.

The older cop drops his head. It's hard to say if he's angry or ashamed.

Officer Hairy Turd fumbles the buttons on a phone and sputters into the receiver, "Ms. Strangeways is here to see you, Chief." Her nose flares at whatever her superior is saying.

She hangs up and directs me toward a cheap vinyl seat outside a glassed-in room with several breaks in the blinds. The openings allow me to see that the Mystick Police Chief is a forty-something Amazon of a Gray Goddess in a transparent blouse, unbuttoned well beyond business standards. After a couple of minutes of yelling into the phone, the chief bursts out the door, hand extended to me like a sword.

"I'm Lara Oakley. Please come in and have a seat, Ced——."

I interrupt her. "The name is Snowy."

Officer Burd snickers behind me.

The fact that Lara started to say my old birth name shows she remembers me. She shoos Mary away and offers me another sticky vinyl chair beside her dented metal desk. Half a dozen awards for crime solving sit atop her putty-colored cabinet. I want to spit on them because she never solved Mom's case.

"How can I help you?" she asks.

"Actually, I'm here to help you," I offer.

She laughs weakly for a woman of her size and occupation. "Really?" she says. "That would be great because I've been feeling like crap."

I harrumph. "You're screwed on the health front, on account of your profession. Investigating murders poisons the body and soul. Your mind is also a mess. Your sheer white blouse and black pants reflect your limited binary view of the universe. Thieves, murderers and demons sit on one side of your world; angels, saints, and you, sit on the other."

A swirling image of black, red, and white squares fills my head, followed by a flash of a bedroom with a white rug, black satin sheets, and red lingerie draped on a chair.

I shake it away and continue, "Even your home is Mob Chic, with plenty of blood tones, like that red-hot bra you're wearing." I point to her cleavage. "And you wonder why you have nightmares?"

She closes two buttons on her blouse. "I see that living in New York City has only sharpened your devilish tongue."

I swirl a finger before her, conjuring. "Later tonight, following our discussion of my mom's messy murder, after you've swigged down a couple shots of Jameson, you'll regret any blood red accents."

She folds her arms over her chest. "Ms. Strangeways, do you actually have anything to offer on Rebekah's case?"

"Yes. Something happened at Slaney's funeral." I hold her skeptical gaze. "A man on the rooftop of the Silver Moon yelled, 'Do as you must,' the same words I found written on Mom's dead body. I couldn't chase him down because I stopped to help a Gray who collapsed in front of me."

"*You* stopped to help someone?" She chuckles. "It would seem you have changed. In any case, there was nothing written on Rebekah Strangeways' corpse. You were quite young when your Mom died. You misremembered several aspects of the crime scene."

"Misremembered?" My face burns. "That's *your* problem, not mine. I know what I saw." I grab my neck and make a slicing motion. "Mom's throat was cut with a jagged blade." I remove my shoes. "Her clogs were flipped over, like so." I grab a piece of paper and a paperclip, write on it, clip it to my shirt, and say. "The words 'Do as you must' were written in blood on her chest. Plenty more of her blood was spilled on the floor."

Lara points to her neck. "You're right about the neck wound." She pulls the paper off my chest. "But you're wrong on the other two counts." She kicks my shoes. "No one tampered with her clogs. There was no writing on the deceased's body. Plus, you neglected to mention that some of the blood on the floor was your own. You're confused because you're worn out from your grandmother's funeral. Funerals are tough, as you know."

I push my chair closer. "No, I don't fricking know. Slaney's funeral is the first one I've attended."

"My apologies," murmurs Laura. "I forgot that your Mom didn't have a funeral. It was written into her last will and testament that she wanted it that way."

"Sure it was." I scoot my chair around to the back of her desk. "That must be an interesting document, a will written by a twenty-five-year-old woman with no health problems, no money, no possessions, and no nurturing, maternal instincts. I'd sure like to see it." I lean an elbow on her desk.

Lara opens her top drawer, removes a bottle of pills, and dry-swallows one. "Rebekah Strangways's will wasn't part of our investigation. You might ask your Aunt Selkie about it, although she may not remember. She has a tendency to forget things that disturb her, just like you."

I move in closer. "Exactly what do you think I've forgotten?"

She shuffles through some files. "For one thing, you've forgotten that your mom traveled with a nasty crowd."

I rock my head back and forth. "Are you saying Mom got what she deserved because she was a pasta-toot?"

"A what?"

I slap the air. "Never mind. I've heard all the rumors about how Mom's free-spirited sex life got her killed. We both know that's small-town bullshit. Don't we?"

I stare her down, hard, remembering what Riley said about my eyes being able to catch any creature, be it fish, fowl, angel or devil.

"You never arrested anyone for Mom's murder, did you?" I ask.

Lara swallows again, as if the pill she took only made it halfway down her throat. "I questioned Riley Finch. But there wasn't any solid evidence linking him to the murder, never mind the kidnapping."

My face twists, confused. "Why would Riley want to kill Mom?" I picture him proudly captaining Slaney's barge.

Laura grunts. "Remember, you were a kid when all this played out. The grownups kept things from you. For instance, Slaney experienced her first bout with cancer around the time your mom died. Rebekah was Slaney's heir, unless something happened to both her and Rebekah. Then, Riley was next in line to inherit Mermaid Cottage."

I squint. "How do you know the details of Slaney's first will?"

"We used to be good friends." Her jaw twitches.

"Why would she choose Rebekah, as heir, over her older daughter, Selkie."

Lara snorts, disgusted. "We both know the answer to that."

I picture the day I caught Selkie downing a bottle of vodka while she was pregnant with Moira and rambling about how she was spawning a demon seed like her mother did with Rebekah.

"Fair enough," I say. "When did Slaney remove Riley from her will?"

"Right after the incident with Amani."

I point to my eye. "The day Alse Critchley took out his eye with her cane. The day you failed to arrest her."

"Alse skipped town."

I consider grabbing Laura's neck but pull myself back. "Well, she's back in town, now. Go arrest her!"

"I can't. The statute of limitations has run on her assault. On the other hand, the statute is not up on your mom's murder."

"Who else had motive to kill Mom?" I ask, frustrated.

Lara rises from her desk, wheezing, as if she's been working out. "Rebekah had many enemies. For one thing, she was blackmailing Clancy."

"Aunt Selkie's husband? Why?"

Lara reaches for her drawer again and then lets go, as if thinking better of it. "Rebekah was sleeping with Clancy. He broke off the affair so as not to upset his alcoholic pregnant wife. Selkie was in her forties and the pregnancy was wearing on her. Clancy was afraid to risk the healthy birth of his only child. He was obsessed with Moira even before she was born. But rumor had it your selfish mother planned to reveal their sleazy relationship to Selkie. Clancy feared his wife might go berserk which gave him motive to kill Rebekah. He may seem like a fun guy. But I think we can both agree that Clancy O'Connor is forever irresponsible, self-centered, and often, quite cruel."

"Clancy and Mom?" I grab my hair. "Please don't tell me that Clancy is my dad!"

"Ha! You're tripping down the wrong trail, there."

"But Clancy could have killed Mom?"

"Sure."

I peer through the broken spots in the blinds and catch Officer Mary Bird spying on us. The fact that she's rubbing her neck makes me smile. She's remembering how I tried to strangle her the day I caught her sitting next to my crush, Brian Cavanaugh, at lunch. Fact is, I would have killed her, if our teacher, Mrs. Sheehan, hadn't duct-taped my hands behind my back.

This memory brings the issue of jealousy to mind. "Lara, why wasn't Selkie your number one suspect? Maybe she found out Mom was sleeping with her husband. That would have given her a great motive to kill Rebekah."

Lara bursts out laughing and spins her desk chair around. "Selkie Strangeways O'Connor, a killer? She is a mental and physical weakling. Plus, she was super-pregnant with Moira at the time of your Mom's murder. Do you think she could have killed anyone?"

I feel my head ache. "Maybe. Was anyone else I know a suspect?"

She harrumphs. "You mean, other than you? You were the one the evidence pointed to. Why do you think we kept calling you in for questioning? We hoped you'd confess. The evidence I had on Riley was circumstantial. I had nothing concrete on Clancy or Selkie. You left your footprints in Rebekah's blood. Your running shoes were a perfect match." She raises an eyebrow and eyes my feet. "Much easier to trace than heels. You also had motive. We all know Rebekah sucked as a mom. No one would blame you if you lashed out at her." Lara narrows her eyes, conveying fake sympathy..

I experience a flashback of a graying brunette police officer who wore the same mask of fake concern. She was the first person to arrive at Mom's murder scene. The woman promised me that my grandma would soon return from her Gray meeting, downtown. But I corrected her, explaining that Slaney was in The City, visiting Fríða. She shushed me and told me to take a nap, while we waited for the ambulance to pick up Mom's body. The whole time, I squeezed my wampum feather necklace from Gertie.

Worse memories follow. I see myself swinging my fists at the cops, while paramedics haul Mom's corpse away. A second ambulance crew arrives to strap me down and shuttle me to a different hospital. I return home a week later to find a "For Sale" sign in front of Monster House. It's been up ever since. People in town say Rebekah's death cursed the place. But that makes no sense. Why would her death curse Monster House and not Mermaid Cottage, which was the place where she died?

Memories of that day stir my blood. "I'm going to find out who wasted Mom, without your help," I announce, seeing myself out.

I head back toward Main Street, where there will be plenty of Grays for me to interrogate. My arms and legs start to itch. Pink welts the size of coffee lids erupt all over my skin. I scratch them and wonder if its nervous hives or I'm allergic to something I ate or drank or touched. My money is on those nasty vinyl seats at the police station or the seaweed tea. I feel more lumps form on my cheeks. I race toward the public bathroom near the drawbridge.

Dozens of Grays stare at me. I'd stare too, if I saw a sweaty girl with white hair, black eyes, and lumpy pink polka dotted skin, wearing studded red stilettos and a marigold mini skirt, running through the middle of this old fashioned New England town.

The public bathroom is packed. A line snakes out onto the street. The Grays take one look at me and wave me to the front of the line. I thank them and splash cold water on my face. I lift my white bangs to dry my pink-welted forehead and what I see beneath them makes my eyes pop. The narrow band of exposed toad brown roots at my scalp has turned a shocking ratsnake gray. I try to blink away what I'm seeing. My hair can't belong to some old woman. It would make more sense for eight-year-old Moira to go gray than it does for me. At least, she loves the Gray lifestyle.

The Grays whisper, as I exit the bathroom. I swear they can smell my newfound old lady scent. They blow kisses at me as I pass.

What the hell is this all about?

I tell myself, *Good God, get a grip, girl. Go back to New York, touch up your roots at some uptown salon and never think about Mystick again.* But I can't do that because I can't let Lara Oakley believe I'm a maniacal mom-killer. I need to prove that what I say happened on the day of Mom's murder is real.

I open my handbag to search for the pills I've used to get me through the last week. My hands shake like a Gray's. I flip through receipts, chewing gum, sparkle eye shadow, opalescent eyeliner, false eyelashes, and matte peach lip stain. No pills. I must have packed them. Then I uncover something shiny, something better than drugs. Lyr Corby's business card gleams up at me like the full moon. A job with Lyr would fund my stay, here, to dig deeper into Mom's murder.

It looks like I have a house to design!

CHAPTER 4
GRANITE HOUSE

Three ruffian crows caw at one another, from their perch atop the sign for Granite House. It hangs off two rusted chains screwed into the lowest branch of a grandfather elm at the top of High Street. Gertie used to say crows gather in threes so one can look ahead, one can attend to current business, and one can keep an eye on the past. Slaney put an Irish eye on these creatures, claiming they signify the presence of the Crow goddess, Macha, who can bring war and peace but leans toward the former.

The girth of the old growth trees on this hilltop reminds me of Gertie's description of the sacred Tree of Life, how its thick roots represent tribal ancestors, its wide trunk symbolizes the living tribe, and its hearty branches denote the next generation of children—something I'll never have. Selkie, Mom, and Slaney neglected their kids. I refuse to screw up another generation of Strangeways.

I head down the tree-lined trail and inhale the fresh earthy woodland scent which somehow reminds me of childhood. The verdant canopy overhead is crowned with giant chestnuts and elms that kiss the sky. My teacher at Mystick Elementary told me those tree varieties were extinct in New England due to blight and disease. Yet they appear hearty here, as if nothing has changed since 1637.

A growl emerges from behind a garage-sized boulder. It can't be a bear. There are no bears in Mystick. Right? Then again, I didn't know about this secret forest, either. I panic and bolt down the path, white hair flying behind me. After sprinting past a second boulder, I spot what looks like a two-story tomb or some kind of historic prison. The front door is made from a single hinged slab of granite.

Granite House!

I ring a brass bell on a hook by the door. It makes a jarring dinner bell kind of sound. The stones above the door are cut in an ocean wave pattern and triangular-shaped stones top the two front windows. One is turned up and the other down. Slaney used to say that when the peak is on top, like a witch's hat, it represents wise old women, and that down-turned triangles represent the life-giving power young women carry within, the power that women in my family always misuse.

As I turn to glance behind me to make sure nothing large with big teeth decided to follow me, the heavy stone door screeches open. Before me stands a tiny woman with hair dyed plum and shaved above her ear on one side and hanging below her chin in a lavender shade on the other. This is the same flossy woman who was quarreling with Fríða at Slaney's funeral.

"Greetings, Snowy. I am Lyr." She lowers her eyelids which are painted with three stacked multicolored lines. "Granite House welcomes you."

"Thank you. I believe you know my guardian, Fríða Olafsdottir," I offer.

"Indeed. Fríða and I have a longstanding professional association. I used to spend a great deal of time in Manhattan. Oh, how I miss it."

Lyr scowls at my chartreuse leather miniskirt but softens when she sees my bejeweled ankle wrap stilettos. "How stunning! Your shoes come from The City, of course."

I raise a finger to my eye. "I was thinking the same thing about your eyeliner."

She surveys my eyes. "You appear to have a great deal of experience with fabulous makeup, yourself." Lyr takes hold of my elbow and leads me beyond the cold stone foyer. "Your artful urbane sensibilities will serve you well, in the years to come."

I blush at the thought that I may have overdone my makeup because I was expecting to see Kai. But then, I always overdo my makeup, thanks to my nannies. My eyes dart around the house, searching for him.

Lyr pats my arm, as if reading my thoughts. "The young man is not presently at home."

I lean into her. "I'm actually glad to hear that. I prefer viewing people's personal space when they're away." I struggle to maintain a professional face and suppress my glee.

"Why?" she wonders.

I raise a coy eyebrow. "The act of making an unbidden intrusion into people's inner sanctums stimulates my designing mind."

"How fascinating! Kai mentioned that he found you to be quite the wonder. I do concur."

Lyr directs me to a sitting room. She makes a face like she has eaten a bad clam and points out two boxy mud-brown chairs and a thuggish maple case that blocks the window facing the river.

"These came with the house," she drones.

"How ghastly," I say, "not to mention odd. Considering Mystick Grays generally adore lithe furniture and airy water views, the location and style of this maple case, in particular, make no sense at all."

"Ombudswomen deviate from Gray norms," she justifies.

I examine the contents of the case. "It's filled with ancient knives and hatchets, like it belongs in a men's hunting club."

Lyr shades her eyes, as if she prefers to shun the cabinet's contents. "Those weapons are, shall we say, the dismal souvenirs of a bygone era. But one must live with one's family heirlooms and honor them, however ghastly. Still, I wish I never had to see them, again."

I gulp at the sight of a leather binder, just below the weapons. It's quite like the one carried by the shouting man on the roof. "What is the purpose of this binder?" I ask.

Lyr leans in and fiddles with the roots of my hair. "Hey!" I protest.

"It is all right, dear. I merely needed to confirm that you have turned gray so I can truthfully answer your question. This binder contains the Rede. The word means "counsel." It is the law of the Gray Goddesses. The Gray Wolves and Gray Foxes follow a different law called the *Qutuhikan*, which means 'the line that cannot be crossed.' The *Qutuhikan* remains unwritten and passed on by word of mouth. Because I have colonial and Pequot ancestry, I am able to represent all four Gray groups as their ombudswoman."

"All four? I only know of the Wolves, Foxes, and Goddesses."

"We do not advertise our fourth group. They are called the Silver Sirens. They live in the posh section of town known as The Borough. Or rather, their boat is docked there. They are not allowed to set foot on land."

"Are they prisoners?"

"Yes, of their own misguided ways."

The pained expression on Lyr's face persuades me to let go of this line of inquiry. I pat the case. "I understand about your family's heirloom weapons. But must you keep this awful albatross-of-a-cabinet as well?

"Yes, it must remain overlooking the river," she sighs, "according to Gray tradition."

Design ideas explode inside my head. "Perhaps, I can cover it with a sort of open-weave chainmail made of copper, bronze, polymer, and steel filament."

"Bravissima!" she raises a small fist. "Then those old weapons will become barely visible, as if viewed through the weighty veil of war and patriarchy that engendered them."

"Thus transforming them from objects of subjugation into object lessons," I finish her sentence.

"Well played and envisioned, Snowy."

"Thank you,Lyr. My grandma, Slaney, taught me that a good designer must see all the possibilities," I wink.

Lyr takes my hands warmly. "You are an exceptional creature, Ms. Strangeways. I cannot wait to hear what you have to say about the rest of this house."

She leads me into the dining room, where screaming tropical colors provoke a blinding headache. These over-the-top shades put Alse's downtown Brazilian murals to shame.

"First," I assess, "these chairs are too tall for this low ceiling. The table is too wide for the space, and the colors are a freak show."

Lyr grabs one of the chairs to steady herself, "Never forget what you just said about these colors. One must never succumb to artistic extremes." She shoots me a poisonous eye. "Beware the Gray Curse. It's first symptom is an obsession with brilliant colors."

I recall Slaney and Rebekah arguing over the paint palette for Monster House, right before Mom's murder. As Supreme Gray Goddess, Slaney would have been obligated to caution any Gray who exhibited a symptom of that curse, even if it was her own daughter.

"Fear not, Ms. Corby," I salute her. "New York neutrals and simple primaries are my stock and trade."

"I'm glad to hear you articulate such safe design boundaries. Vigilance is the best defense against The Gray Curse. Just remember that we have a fine Gray rehabilitation facility in Brazil, should you ever need it." She swirls a finger at my chartreuse skirt.

I don't get a chance to explain the overly-colorful skirt is a designer hand-me-down from my overly-colorful nannies because my throat tightens the moment we step into her kitchen.

""Shall we gut this dark wood Hansel and Gretel nightmare?" I ask Lyr.

She flashes nails manicured like the skin of a rattlesnake. "Absolutely! The woods around this house contain good spirits and these interiors must reflect that."

I toss her a thumbs up. "Consider it as good as gone," I say, neglecting to mention that I never design kitchens.

Lyr's fabulous eyes drift up the curved flight of stairs. "There is a painting by one of your relatives, on the second floor. Perhaps I can purchase one of yours to go with it. Then I would own 'A Set of Strangeways,'" she simpers.

I ignore her lame joke about my surname, having heard them all. "My paintings are amateurish," I demure, recalling how Fríða never allowed my artwork to grace her refrigerator when I was a kid.

Lyr wrinkles a well-penciled brow as we mount the stairs. "I admire the fact that you judge your work by global standards. Much of what passes for art around here is seaside schlock. You are right to stand above the provincial tastes of the Mystick Gray Goddesses. Force them to look up to you. Demonstrate your elevated status with worldly designs."

Considering how much I bash Slaney's Shipwreck Chic, I'm surprised to find myself horribly insulted, on behalf of my hometown artists. "You are a sophisticated woman, Lyr," I suck up. "I understand why you distance yourself from the rank and file Grays. I'd already be back in The City, if I didn't need to look into Mom's murder."

She stiffens. "Indeed, your mother's death was a dark business. To counter such darkness, one must seek light— the heart of all great art, design, and noble living." She points to a shiny yellow brass door at the top of the stairs that almost gleams. "Shall we?"

"It looks like something out of the Italian Renaissance," I exclaim.

"You possess a keen eye," she grins. "It is a replica of the famed door from the Baptistery in Florence." She opens it and gestures for me to enter. "Let us take a peek at the Strangeways' painting I mentioned. Shall we?"

I go limp when I see what she's talking about. It's a portrait of a woman's head with graying toad brown hair and crow black eyes. The tops and sides of the head are cut off by a tightly boxed frame. Her features are painted in thick, rash, disappointed strokes, emphasizing her wide elliptical eyes, rough triangular nose, and awkward hexagonal lips, all tinted in a raging inferno of burning oranges, yellows and reds, punctuated by slashes of charcoal. This face belongs to a long-suffering woman, easily identified as my mom, Rebekah Strangeways.

"I never saw Slaney paint with such bold strokes, before," I rasp. "Never mind capture such complex geometry and color in her portraiture."

"Of course not, Snowy. This is your mother's art, not Slaney's. Her work was always far edgier. How might you complement this piece by Rebekah with your own décor?" she pries.

"M-my mom painted this?" I rub my eyes.

"Indeed! It certainly reflects the constraint she felt, living in Mystick."

"Mom is beginning to sound like my clone." I count on my fingers. "First, she doesn't get along with her mother. Second, she feels trapped, here. Third, she paints hopeless people. I should tell you that my last painting showed an old Manhattan woman watering her dead plants. I hope I'm not becoming my mom."

Lyr's tricolor eyelids lower. "We all become our mothers. We are also very much our own women. Women are multifaceted creatures. Don't forget that."

I can't pull my eyes away from this tormented image of Mom.

Lyr coos, "Perhaps you need time to process the emotions this painting conjures. Do you wish to reconsider taking on this house project?"

Sensing a much-needed contract slipping away, I shoot my ideas out, rapid-fire. "I already have wonderful plans for Granite House. To complement Rebekah's artwork, I'd echo the shapes and colors of her facial features in geometric primary color furnishings. The walls would carry a neutral taupe, allowing those colors to pop." I point to the side of the room. "Here, I'd place an elliptical yellow bed. Beside it, a red hexagonal side table." I gesture to the opposite wall, "A blue parallelogram mirror would go right here, creating a composition of bold but balanced geometric elements like you'd find in a Kandinsky painting."

Lyr's face illuminates. "Ah, Kandinsky." She folds her hands and appears to drift into a memory. "Such a brilliant man. I was so young when we enjoyed that one, brief kiss. Our age difference was simply too great to bridge." She blushes. "It would seem that you and I share the same loves." Lyr pulls herself up to her full five feet and stretches overhead to grip my towering shoulders. "Snowy Strangeways, you are just the gal to drag Granite House out of the Stone Age."

I place my hands on hers. "We will call this room 'Kandinsky's Kiss?'"

The tears welling up in Lyr's eyes tell me that I've just clinched this design deal. She leads me down the stairs less steadily than she mounted them.

"We can view the rest of Granite House the next time you visit," she excuses. "Feel free to change anything you like, except the weapon's case and the name of this house. Beyond those restrictions, I trust your judgment. You may do as you . . ." She breaks into a cough. "Do as you see fit."

My heart pounds at hearing her start to say the words that were written on Mom's chest.

Lyr catches my spirits falling, and suggests, "Shall we examine Kai's wing before you go?"

I follow her to a back door of the house that opens onto a corridor, leading to a small annex. "Kai must have held killer high school parties, living this far away from his mom," I observe.

"Certainly not!" Lyr argues. "His friends were not allowed on this property. My work is highly confidential."

"No friends? No parties? Are you serious? When was this corridor and addition installed?"

"I had it built two decades ago, for my son and his nanny."

"You've lived in separate buildings since Kai was a child?"

"We've lived in separate buildings since the day I adopted him." Lyr stops at the door to fumble with a chain around her neck to access the right key.

"You raised him like a puppy in a doghouse," I gaffe.

Lyr's lips curl as she unlocks Kai's door. "Snowy Strangeways, you, of all people, should understand my lack of a nurturing instinct. Your grandmother gave Barnacle Bill to Riley Finch, a man with whom she had a severe falling out, because you—her sole heir—weren't nurturing enough. You and I are not cat people or kid people. We are designing creatures of a different breed. Besides, my dear Snowy, there are some things in this world far worse than missing pajama sleepovers and pin the tail on the donkey games. I have protected Kai from those things."

Other than cannibals, vampires, zombies, and Windigos, I can't imagine what in hell she thinks she protected him from. Then something hits me—HARD.

"What's wrong, dear?" asks Lyr.

I lower my head. "My upbringing wasn't that different from Kai's. No other kids my age wanted to talk about wallpaper designs, drapery fabrics, fascias and patinas. Adult designers and exotic dancers were my only friends. Víðsýni's showroom took up all of Fríða's building, except for her tiny bedroom and small living area. My bedroom was located on the third floor of Hips, next door. I was also a puppy who lived outside. But my outside world was happy. Like all big events in my life, my sixteenth birthday party was celebrated with my nannies. They invited New York's top drag queens to serenade me with a sizzling rendition of "Only Sixteen." Then they took me on an upholstery fabric buying spree in the Garment District. I wouldn't trade that memory for anything."

Lyr sighs. "Gray children lead colorful, if not fully-parented, lives."

Traveling the corridor between Kai and Lyr's residences, we pass metal animal sculptures, assembled from machine parts. They include a black bear, deer, turkey, porcupine and rabbit. Kai's name is etched on each of them.

"Your son made these?" I ask, dazzled.

"Indeed, Kai was not without teenage diversions. He created these sculptures in high school, drawing artistic inspiration from the creatures of these woods. In college, he began spending more time working as an investigative journalist. In the end, growing up in My-stick around Gray women who keep so many secrets made him more curious than creative. You seem to have mastered both tendencies."

I force myself to let that remark slide and reexamine the bear sculpture with a shudder, recalling the growling sound I heard outside.

She tosses open the door to Kai's living quarters and crinkles her fabulous eyes. "Voila!"

My eyes widen. "This is one hell of a doghouse!"

I note the predictable retro-journalist items:

One roll-top desk with a brass banker's lamp. Check.

One signed photograph of famed Watergate journalists Woodward and Bernstein. Check. One drawer filled with newspaper typeset letter blocks. Check.

One fluffy white bed. Yum.

Lyr taps on the framed document over the headboard which brings me back to our conversation.

"Wow! This looks like an original account of John Peter Zenger's eighteenth century libel trial," I assess. "Considering Zenger was the first great American journalist. I'll bet Kai worships him."

Lyr clears her throat, "My son received this document as an anonymous gift on his twenty-first birthday."

"An anonymous gift?" My curiosity radar pops up. "Kai mentioned that he was adopted. Was this gift from his biological mom?"

"I can't say," she offers, dismissively.

I drop this touchy line of inquiry, remembering Lyr is my only potential client, and quickly segue. "Everyone in this town appears to be pursuing the dream of a world gone by. Kai wants to be an old-time journalist. You are burdened with that awful case of relics. I'm stuck with my grandma's archaic decorating business, at least until some enterprising Gray Goddess makes me a decent offer."

Lyr 's face remains glued to the Zenger document, as if she's caught inside a memory. Or could it be a vision? I pick up the archaeology magazine lying on Kai's bed and see it's bookmarked to an article on women's naked river-bathing rituals.

I place it in front of Lyr's dazed face. "It looks like the skinny-dipping Grays at Slaney's funeral peaked Kai's curiosity."

She regains focus. "It's my son's job as a journalist to be curious about the leading women of his town, even when some of them act like irresponsible fools. We have worked hard to remain below the radar of our enemies."

Her face enlivens as she scans the room. "I hate to admit it, but his 1920s style brings me back to my childhood."

"Very funny," I chortle. "I'm guessing you were born closer to the Second World War."

"Certainly not. I am nearly a centenarian."

"C'mon. Your seventy-five, at most."

"Add a couple of decades. Ombudswomen live long lives, perhaps because we do not suffer mates."

"Neither my mom nor grandma suffered mates much past reproduction. But even that small sufferance may have resulted in their undoing. I don't know the name of my father or grandfather."

"Alas, that is the Gray way."

I'm stuck on the miracle of Lyr's youthful appearance. "There's no way you can be as old as you claim. I don't see a single wrinkle. Can I snoop inside your medicine cabinet and check out the labels on your skin care products?"

Her tone turns somber. "Once you begin work on the Granite House interiors, this entire house will be available for your full inspection, from skin creams to ductwork."

"Are we leaving Kai's newspaper shrine alone? Or is his room also up for a redesign?"

"Let it be," she moans. "This house comes and goes with my job.

Kai will not be living here for long. He and his fiancé, Brook Beemer, will soon need to find a place of their own. They will surely make their home in Mystick. That girl will never leave this antiquated town. She has studied Gray rituals since before she could walk. She may even lead the Gray Goddesses, one day."

I process this news that Kai and Brook have planned a Mystick happily ever after.

Lyr pets my well-styled hair. "I see you are just as displeased as I am about Kai's impending nuptials with little Ms. Mystick. But there's nothing to be done about it. My only hope is that he tires of her before she ditches him, as all Gray women do their men."

She holds my strained face in her hands. "If Kai was seeing someone like you, he might be bold enough to visit exotic locales and uncover Pulitzer Prize-winning stories. Alas, those hopes are in vain. We both know you have a great future ahead of you, a future which does not include dating small town journalists."

My throat swells. "Where is Kai now?"

Lyr leads me back through the hall of metal animal sculptures. "My dear, I don't know. Brook called me this morning to say she was unable to reach him. But I don't want to get my hopes up, even if it would be too wonderful to discover that he has tossed her and her wretched clogs to dash off somewhere fascinating."

I shake Brook and Kai out of my head because this is the moment that Lyr and I cut a business deal, or not.

"How shall we proceed with your interior design work, Ms. Corby?" I hide my sweaty palms. "Due to my age, my legal contracts must still go through Fríða at Víðsýni. I know that's a nuisance but I'm not yet licensed."

"I do not need a formal contract or license," she inserts. "This job can stay off the books. It is yours if you want it, my dear. You may begin right away. Feel free to set your own price for the work."

"My own price?"

"Absolutely. I have a long history with the Strangeways."

CHAPTER 5
MONSTER HOUSE

Yes, I'm resentful. No, I've never met her. But I know Brook's kind. Eyes like the ocean. Hair like the sun. Friends like the characters in a Hallmark television show. A well-painted white colonial house with a cantankerous tabby cat that has licked her perfect pink cheeks since birth.

I pass the houses on River Road that I nicknamed as a kid. There's Creepy Caspar, the poorly whitewashed house that disappears into the surrounding foliage at twilight; the Woodchopper's Cabin, a rustic whitewashed home, surrounded by a thicket of pines and untamed shrubberies, owned by two burly old women who love to heft axes and maintain a sky-high woodpile; Scary Snow White, the milk-colored colonial with the blood red door, electric blue shudders and raven roof; Rabid Fan, the flat white saltbox with the New England sports logos on its mailbox, windows, doors, and cars. But I know Brook's kind. distracts me from watching where I'm walking.

A squealing sound and the smell of burnt rubber brings me back. I find myself facing the bumper of a cherry-red Chevy pickup that has pulled out of the house that I call "Captain America" an eggshell-painted federal with an oversized golden eagle plaque and gigantic American flag out front. The truck bumper rests inches from my chest. I'm lucky to be alive.

A rod-straight woman in a Coast Guard captain's uniform jumps out of the driver's seat and removes her cap. "I'm so sorry. Are you all right?"

I fix my crow black eyes on this woman who nearly killed me. "You're the owner of 'Captain America."

"Pardon me?" she says.

I point to her home. "This is your place?"

"Yes, ma'am."

"You sleep in a bed with a headboard painted with the image of a Coast Guard cutter. Right?"

"How could you know that?" She slips back into her truck.

As a Coast Guard officer, she's faced rogue waves, desperate drug lords, and pirate scares on the high seas; yet my visions are too much.

I grin at the orange-headed twin girls who duck down into the floor of the back seat. "Hey guys!" I say. "I bet you have bunk beds shaped like boats, and your mom painted your walls the same gray-green as the icy waters of Long Island Sound."

The twins whimper like puppies. One of them holds her phone screen up over the seat. There's a picture of some electronic creature on it with long tentacles that she's using to ward me off.

"Young woman," the captain brusques. "I'm glad you're okay. But we're late for soccer practice." She hits the gas, veers her car around me, and escapes in a cloud of dirt.

I continue walking toward Mermaid Cottage at a faster pace and pass my Aunt Selkie's overly-tartaned home, which I call the Mad House of Plaid. Then I round the bend to the Woodchopper's Cabin. My stilettoed feet feel like they're on fire. I rest on the curb near the cabin, rubbing them, stalling, trying to compose myself before turning the corner to Monster House. I'm still rubbing them when the larger of the woodchopper women emerges hefting an axe in one hand and a pair of clogs in the other.

I ward her off. "Oh, hell on hot rollers no!" I refuse. "I promised myself, long ago, that I would never dress like a Gray."

I jam my sore feet back into my stilettos, toss the woodswoman a farewell salute, and press on to Monster House.

A flash of crimson paint appears before my eyes. Then more colors and shapes burst into my head like a psychedelic acid trip. This happens every time I'm here. Yet the colors never transform into anything lucid. I suffer an eternal block about the interiors of this house. My visions never result in anything concrete.

Blinking away my vision, what I see next makes the heels of my stilettos jam into the pavement like emergency brakes. A shiny new "SOLD" banner covers the worn "For Sale" sign that's hung in front of Monster House for the last eight years. I blink twice to be sure what I'm seeing is real. The Monster has been lifeless since Mom died. I need to know who resurrected it. I decide to call my Aunt Selkie because she frequents Our Lady of the River, Catholic Church, where gossip is never in short supply. I wish I had a cell phone, as I briskly hobble inside Mermaid Cottage on my much-abused stilettoed feet.

"Good afternoon, Aunt Selkie," I huff into the receiver.

"Well if it isn't Ms. Fancypants from The City," she says. "Clancy hasn't served me with divorce papers yet, if that's what you're calling about." Her voice skips, as though she has been crying.

"That's good news. Isn't it?" I estimate, knowing she's a religious woman.

"I suppose so," she heaves. "How are you enjoying your inheritance from my mother?"

I consider slapping her with the news that Slaney once picked Riley Finch to inherit ahead of her but think better of it.

"I just successfully pitched a new design job," I say, hoping to assert my superior work ethic. "I'm sorry to hear things are not going well with Clancy."

She snarls on the other end of the phone, "If 'not going well' is the term you young gals use to describe a husband who's run off on you for the hundredth time, then I'd sure say they're not going well. He should know better than to keep sniffing skirts at his age."

I recall what Lara said about Clancy's affair with Rebekah and don't bite. "I have some stunning news. Perhaps you've already heard it. The house next door sold."

"Not The Monster?" she gasps.

"Yes," I reply, surprised that she calls the house the same thing I do.

Selkie tisks. "Pity the buyer. No good can come of that place."

"I'm curious to know who's moving in."

"Not too curious, I hope." She clucks into the receiver, assuming the role of the responsible auntie, dissuading her niece from pulling the trigger on her nosiness addiction. "You should call *Mystick Lights* newspaper. They'll have the information regarding the land transaction and purchase. That way, you won't need to pry and get yourself into your usual trouble." She hangs up on me.

The "usual trouble" to which she is referring is ancient history. A few days before Mom's murder, I broke into an abandoned downtown Mystick mansion that was scheduled for demolition because I heard it housed an extraordinary mural. It never occurred to me that anyone cared whether or not a ten-year-old kid viewed an important piece of local artwork that was about to be lost forever. Once I viewed the mural, I didn't care about getting caught. It depicted a riverscape that wasn't ridiculously bright like Alse's tropical murals or deathly dull like some of Slaney's designs. This mural showed the Mystick riverscape in the days before the Mayflower. Vibrant, crystal-clear water teamed with sturgeon and alewives. Eagle's nests overlooked chestnut bark-covered wigwams. Foxes, wolves, deer, turkey, and black bears roamed the woods in healthy numbers. A sense of peace hung over this world. This artist must have had her feet deeply planted in the Mystick mud.

Viewing that mural would have been enough to make the break-in worth it. But I also discovered a basement workroom that reminded me of a chef's kitchen, except it lacked a stove. I opened the freezer and found glass sheets covered in dabs of organic paint. I'd heard of freezing paint palettes to keep natural paint fresh but never seen it done. I also found a padlocked trunk. I concentrated on remotely viewing its contents but received no clear vision, just a chaotic brain blast of color. I found a crowbar and wedged it into the padlock, prying hard. It wouldn't budge. I kept trying, until a bright flashlight shone in my eyes, and a police officer faced me, with her revolver drawn.

Slaney fetched me from the police station with her face steaming red. I'd never seen her so mad. She told the officer she didn't need to worry about me snooping around anymore. On the way out, she squeezed my arm hard enough to leave a bruise. The next day, the police phoned to ask how I knew the location of that trunk. They called me a liar when I told them I was only there to view the mural.

The New York City Police Department is nothing like these guys. They leave me alone because they have bigger problems than chasing down juvenile interior designers. Besides, there are plenty of legal ways to snoop in The Big Apple. For one thing, most apartment windows lack curtains or blinds, providing ready junk food for voyeurs. For a heartier viewing feast, I visited the apartments of the recently deceased. Armed with impeccable hair and makeup, short leather skirts and fabulous shoes, landlords were always more-than-ready to open their doors.

Mystick is just the opposite; it's a land of closed curtains. The town's Puritan colonists left their repressive mark. Snooping is only permitted for the police and newspaper reporters. Fortunately, the fact that Monster House is this town's most notoriously vacant property means that Selkie is right; the newspapers have surely been sniffing around about the new buyer.

I dial the number for *Mystick Lights.*

"Newsroom," answers a hoarse male voice.

"Hello. My name is Snowy Strangeways. I'm trying to find out who bought the house next door to mine on River Road?"

The man on the other end clears his throat. "Hey, Snowy! It's me, Kai."

My voice jumps an octave. "Kai! I'm glad I caught you. I live at . . ."

He cuts in. "I know where you live."

"You are quite the prying investigator."

"You have a longstanding reputation for being pretty nosey, yourself."

"Very funny. I see you figured out I'm Slaney Strangeways granddaughter?"

"About halfway through our first conversation."

"Your mom said you went AWOL on your fiancé."

He re-clears the hungover sounding frog in his throat. "Brook Beemer is now my ex-fiancé, thank you very much. That means that my confidential investigative assignment is none of her damn business. Nothing in my life is any of her damn business, anymore."

"It sounds to me like you dumped your woman and then found an excuse to leave town, so you wouldn't have to deal with the ugly fallout. That makes you a jerk."

"Maybe a partial jerk. But you'll be pleased to know that my excuse-of-an-investigation came up with information on your mystery buyer on River Road. I have the name of the new owner. Hold on a second. Let me check if I'm allowed to share it with you before it goes to press."

His chair squeals as he rolls around on old wheels. "Ms. Moon," he says, "is it okay to disclose the buyer of the house on River Road to the next-door neighbor?"

A shudder runs through me when I realize he's talking to *Mystick Lights* Editor Nori Moon. She once wrote an editorial offering her slant on how I killed my mom. I was ten years' old, for God's sake! The week after that article came out, Slaney sent me to Manhattan to live with Fríða.

"Which neighbor?" I hear Nori ask, with her grizzly bear voice. "Is it one of those woodsy lumberjack gals?"

"No, it's Snowy Strangeways, from Mermaid Cottage."

"Oh, her," she scoffs. "She won't gossip. She has no friends. I suppose she deserves to know what she's up against, professionally-speaking. Just tell her not to share anything with her blabbermouth Aunt Selkie."

Kai returns to the phone and exhales. "Snowy, I'm sure you heard that. The buyer is Zola Black."

"Very funny, Kai." I snap my fingers a couple of times. "Now tell me the real name of the buyer."

"It's true, Snowy. Zola Black, the reigning queen of interior design just bought the house next door to yours. I'm truly sorry."

I swallow. "Goodbye, my Perhaps Friend. I must now retreat, to meditate on how completely screwed I am."

I collapse onto my kitchen floor and stare up at the ceiling. Brown water stains and hairline cracks mar the old white plaster. Ceilings are the ugliest part of colonial homes. This typical blotchy white mess was the last thing that Mom saw, as her warm red life slipped away from her. She loved color and must have hated this view. What else did Mom see in her final moments? A bright light that led to something better? An endless wormy darkness? Was she thinking about the weird green kitchen she'd started designing at Monster House? Or was it a relief for her to know she'd soon be free of her color obsession and The Gray Curse?

I try not to think about the apocalyptic professional implications of Zola showing up in this town. I wonder how hard Selkie will laugh when she opens her morning paper and sees the news about Zola Black buying Monster House. She will surely light a candle at mass to give thanks that her gold-digging niece can no longer reap a profit from the sale of her mom's interior design business.

I stare out the window at Slaney's stupid mermaid business sign. The contents of my empty stomach slosh around like rough seas. I wish I ordered a better sign as soon as my grandma passed away. I didn't do it because I had no plans to make a personal commitment to her business. I haven't wanted to have anything to do with this town in eight years. So why do I feel a burning rage over this looming threat to Slaney Strangeways, Decorating? Why do I suddenly want to stay here and fight for that business, even if it means running it, myself?

PART II
INTERIOR DESIGNS

Mystick Lights
OPINION
By KAI CORBY

"Gray Lightning Strikes"

"Nobody respects old gray haired gals more than the people of Mystick."
- Zola Black

You've all heard the news: Zola Black—creator of planet Earth's most beloved line of eco-furnishings— just bought a house in our town.For those of you who have been living off-world since the 1900s, this is the woman who injected the shoreline granola crowd with a much-needed shot of panache in the early twenty-first century. Her iconic eco-friend-ly interiors included "White Tiger"—a sleek and cozy line of black and white organic faux fur furniture—and "Dear Rafflesia"—a breathtaking series of large print natural fiber wallpapers and furniture inspired by the humongous leathery flower of the same name. Zola's ramped-up natural interiors are so breathtaking that some have claimed she cut an unholy deal with Mother Nature herself.

For years, this creator of the renowned ZB label has curried her lush design palate at exotic locales, chasing flamingos on Chaxa Lagoon, wrestling with lemurs in Madagascar, and swimming through triple rainbows at Iguazu Falls. But according to a reliable source, there are no more glamorous trips scheduled on Ms. Black's calendar. The great lady has retired. Her only immediate plans are nursing an adorable Somali kitten and redecorating the neglected Victorian house on River Road in our fair town.

This reporter wonders what is behind Zola's shocking shift. Could it be that somewhere in Ms. Black's well-appointed closet there lies a sordid tale of tax evasion, recovering substance abuse, forbidden liaison, or some other spicy tabloid-ready peccadillo? Or perhaps, the great Zola Black is ready to settle into small town life? *Right.*

Stay tuned, Mysticks. It will all come out, eventually. Meanwhile, let's greet our new neighbor with an old-fashioned Mystick welcome. No, I don't mean that you should drown her in pumpkin whoopee pies. Take her out for tea at The Silver Moon. Show her our historic seaport. Suggest a visit to the aquarium. Bring her a jug of our world-renowned cider. Offer her some of our peerless red shrimp and mega-scallops. Don't be stingy Mysticks! Share our treasures with your new neighbor!

Ms. Black, whatever brings you here, we know you'll love our unique town, where the long gray-haired gals always run the show!

CHAPTER 6
DO AS YOU MUST

In the week since Zola bought the Monster, my mind has wandered some rocky terrain. I've suffered nightmares about bright green kitchens and heard footsteps coming from my grandma's design barn. Sometimes, I even hear voices, there. This madness must stop. I'm moving the design boards for Granite House out of the cramped space inside Mermaid Cottage and into the barn. If I force myself to work there, this nonsense will surely end.

I reach the sliding barn door, unlock it, and push it sideways. The hinges bump up and down, but the door stays shut. I heave harder, until it rambles open with a thunk. Clearly, no one has opened this thing in a while. I expect the interior to smell musty but the fresh scents of sea salt and Macintosh apples pour out, along with the subtler smells of beeswax, cedar, seaweed, and a hint of patchouli. To breathe in this barn is to inhale the Mystick Gray World.

The ocean blue walls are ringed with thick white candles that are four feet high. The shelves are covered with knotted nautical rope balls, shoreline paintings framed in barn board, colorful deck prisms, piles of quartz crystals, healing herb bundles, humongous seashells, and carved wooden incense burners. Barnacle Bill's boat-shaped cat bed sits in the far-left corner of the room. Looking at that empty bed makes me feel guilty. Why didn't Slaney let me take her cat?

I recall Lyr's words. *Snowy Strangeways, you, of all people, should understand my lack of a nurturing instinct. Your grandmother had to give Barnacle Bill away to Riley Finch, a man with whom she had a severe falling out, simply because you—her sole heir—aren't nurturing enough.*

I want to do something for Slaney. So I set my design boards near the large candles and light them because that is how she reviewed her designs. Slaney claimed firelight makes things come alive. As light and shadows dance across the walls, floor, and boards, I begin to think she may have been correct.

"Lyr," I say, rehearsing my presentation, "my mentor taught me that great designs don't need to be born of love; our demons may be our finest muses. With that in mind, I begin our interior design discussion with your weapons case. As I suggested, we can make this piece less intrusive by covering it with an open weave mixed-metal filament, in a kind of stylized chainmail, and light it from within, so the articles of destruction within it will appear as but a distant nightmare of a dark world gone by."

The candles flicker, offering some encouragement. I shudder at the thought of the leather binder that contains the Rede, the law of the Gray Goddesses. The image of its rich brown leather fixes in my mind, along with that of the man on the roof of the Silver Moon who was holding it and shouting *Do as you must.*

I roll out the kinks in my neck, like the performers at Hips taught me to do, and continue practicing my pitch.

"To complement and balance the male brutishness of this case, we can install wallpaper that features classic images of the Amazonian woman warriors from Homer's Odyssey. I also recommend installing a delicate bow-shaped chandelier, set with flickering bulbs to suggest their flaming arrows, and lean rust-colored furniture with ebony trim reminiscent of Greek vases to replace the boxy brown chairs."

The candle flames sputter like clapping hands.

Feeling more secure, I press on. "A mirrored ceiling and two mirrored walls in the dining room will replicate two walls of forest wallpaper and an evergreen colored glass table top with a bronze trunk base. A crescent-shaped pewter lighting fixture, overhead, will honor the moon's dual place of honor in your home as the Moon Goddess Arianrhod and your Native American Grandmother Moon."

The candles gleam like the midday sun on the Mystick River.

Still, I doubt Lyr will react as brightly to the notable absence of kitchen designs in my presentation. Fríða better give me a straight answer about helping me design that room, when I head to The City to source the items I need for this project.

I sit at Slaney's white crackle-painted desk. Mystick Grays love crackle paint because it makes things look like they've been dragged out to sea and washed ashore. I roll my crackle chair from design board to design board, brooding. Something about this design bothers me. More light might help me see things better.

The scallop-shaped wall sconces with small beeswax candles remind me of the beeswax candle poking out of Slaney's pocket in her self-portrait. I light them and their warm glow draws attention to Slaney's four "Mystick Moira" paintings, depicting my young cousin in each of the four seasons. Moira's summer painting shows her paddling an apple red kayak with her lobster hair piled atop her head. For the winter scene, Moira wears a pine tree sweater and sips cocoa, heaped with whipped cream and Christmas-colored jimmies, while the lighted Winter Boat Parade twinkles behind her on the river. The spring painting depicts her playing with blue crabs in the children's wading pool at the seaport, framed by a nearby bed of daffodils. But it's the fall painting that captures the spirit of this rare child whom people admire and fear. It depicts Moira storming past trees bursting with crimson and gold autumn foliage, blowing her infamous foghorn, dressed in tan tweed, like an Irish baby Godzilla.

This painting is not fanciful. Clancy taught Moira to blow that horn when passing any empty house that might contain evil spirits, or worse, evil people. *Mind you, this is not a legitimate Irish custom. This is pure blarney.* But in all fairness, Clancy invented the practice to give his kid the courage to walk home from school. Tales of what happened to Lucy Wauby and Amani Jones still haunt the kids in this town. The trouble is, that when people hear Moira whistling outside their house, they frenetically rush to flip on their outdoor lights and fling open their front doors, for fear she will think their house empty and set off her horn which sounds like a demon hoard.

How does Moira get away with this outrageous practice?

It isn't because she's pretty; good-looking Irish children are a dime a dozen in Mystick. Moira O'Connor possesses a kind of fay glamour that suggests she deserves her own bard. Her father, Clancy, is much the same. This father-daughter duo's striking looks and hypnotic singing voices have lead the old-timers at the Irish-American Club to joke that the pair descend from the charmed wee folk of the Emerald Isle. Clancy insists that Moira merely carries the O'Connor family's natural gifts, passed down from their ancestor, the great King Conchobhar, born around the time of Jesus Christ.

Clancy's bond with his daughter was forged before birth. When Selkie's ultrasound revealed a healthy female fetus, Clancy claimed he could tell that the child's spirit matched his own. Seeing that prenatal picture also triggered something in Selkie. But it was nothing wholesome. I caught her downing a bottle of vodka and ranting about spawning a demon seed. That was the same day Mom and Selkie had their fight over grandma's banal sense of color.

I force myself to stop procrastinating and write purchase orders for the items I need for Granite House. I'm starting to head-bob with boredom, when an Irish tune floats into my daydream. The sound sends a surge of adrenaline through me, and I rush to throw open the barn door. Before me stands a broad-shouldered man in a yellow slicker that's dripping from the rain. His curls are the color of boiled lobster and his green eyes are as pale as seagrass. His slicker hangs open, which allows me to notice he's better dressed than usual, or rather, over-dressed for July, heaped with layers of woolies and tweeds, including a well-fitted vest and jacket that must have been handed down from another century. His neck is wrapped with three paisley scarves, and his entire overblown ensemble is topped off with a porkpie hat, like he's a walking Donegal suitcase.

"Clancy," I say. "What are you doing here?"

"I'm saying my goodbyes. That's what I'm doing here," he says, wiping rain from his brow.

I survey his rusted pickup truck. The bed is empty, which seems strange for a man on the move.

"I figured you left town after walking out on Selkie. Why have you come to see me?"

He drives his clenched fists into his thighs and rocks his head from side to side. "Well surprise on you. Surprise on me, too. I figured you'd be gone by now. But here we are, both of us, still stuck in bloody Mystick." He shakes his clenched fist at the cloudy sky.

"Don't turn this around," I fold my arms. "I'm still here because I'm looking into Mom's murder. I understand that the two of you had an affair when Selkie was pregnant with Moira."

He waggles a finger. "That would be none of your business, little girl. You're not even old enough to drink."

"I'm not the immature one. You were worried that my mom might tell Selkie about your sketchy relationship. Maybe you were worried enough to kill her."

He whacks me on the head with his hat. "Listen to that fairy tale, will you? It sounds to me like you've fallen victim to your notoriously obsessive curiosity, which can only send you to The Land of Trouble. You are one ill-fated lass." He raises his voice. "Though I suppose anything's better than falling victim to The Gray Curse." He rolls those last words off his tongue in a lingering Irish way that chills my spine.

"It's funny that you should say I'm ill-fated. If I'm not mistaken, the fates are called 'Moira' in Greek. You named your own daughter after them, breaking with the Gray tradition about water names."

His chest puffs up. "You *are* mistaken, woman of the Strangeways. Not everyone on this planet worships the Greeks. I am pleased to inform you that my daughter is, in fact, named for a Gaelic word that means 'bitter,' because bitterness sums up the circumstances of her birth. Your birth was a bitter thing, as well." He shakes his head like you do to ward off a chill. "When you were born, your parents named you Cedar, another non-water name but also a well-chosen one. Cedar is a sacred Native American plant with the power to ward off evil. It was a wise name. But you went and changed it. Sometimes I think the women in your family invite bad luck."

"Actually, I was named after swamp cedar. So it is a water name, albeit a ridiculous one," I correct him.

"And Snowy is not?" He closes one eye.

"It goes along with Selkie and Slaney's names."

"Not really." His eyes drift. "Sláine is the great river of health in Ireland. Selkies are lovely but dangerous shapeshifting seals. Snowy has little to do with the Emerald isle. And don't get me started on your mother, Rebekah, whose name translates to mean a woman who traps a man with her beauty."

I throw up my hands. "Are you even from this century? You blame my dead Mom's good looks for your affair?"

He sits down on the barn doorstep, like he doesn't care about the puddle of water beneath him, and flips his hat between his knees. "Your trouble is, you're not your own woman. You're the one who is obsessed with your mom, not me. You hope to wash away your bitterness by un-covering the truth about her death. Finding the truth may only make you more bitter." His eyes flash. "Don't get me wrong, I wish you well in your search for Rebekah's killer. But you're wasting your time dealing with the local police. Chief Lara Oakley failed to solve Rebekah's case eight years ago, for want of trying. I like her well enough. She's easy on the eyes and soft on the heart. But . . ."

"You are an incorrigible chauvinist. You know that?"

His face twinkles. "Laura's one hell of a woman. But she ain't much of as a cop."

I step out into the drizzle and punch him.

He rubs his arm. "Maybe you killed Rebekah. You are not only an ill-fated lass but also an angry one."

"Despite your stupid sexist remarks about me and Chief Oakley and Mom, I think you may be right about Laura's lousy cop credentials. I've spoken to her about Mom's case and found her semi-useless. Mean-while, will you please explain to me why you're still in Mystick?"

He gazes downriver, toward the ocean. "I'm cleaning up my loose ends, one of which is Selkie." He raises his right hand, as if swear-ing to something. "Skipping out on her was wrong. I know that. But you've seen her nasty habits. There's no light in the woman. I've hooked up with a new gal who is sober and has a bit of dough. My marriage to your aunt is over. I believe in traditional divorce. Brush your hands clean, harbor no hard feelings, and move on. Keep the money-grubbing lawyers out of it, I say." He grunts, "But you know Selkie. If I bring up divorce, she'll start another screaming row and make the coppers happy. You need to convince your aunt to let me take Moira, so I can make a good life for the girl. That's why I came here to see you. The child can't stay with her foul mother. We both know that." He pounds his knuckles together.

It's hard for me not to agree. Most women would not side with a misogynist uncle who has ditched their aunt for some rich broad and plans to steal their kid. But Selkie is not your typical aunt, just as Clancy is not your typical uncle. I've seen Selkie shake Moira too hard, more than once. The rest of the time, she ignores her. On the other hand, Moira would hate to leave Mystick. She loves the Gray lifestyle. She is as much a part of this town as the river.

"I'll encourage Selkie to let you go," I concede. "But I'm leaving custody up to a judge."

He shakes his hat at me. "Why? What happiness have you ever seen the child take from her mother? The wretched woman leaves the girl alone or with a babysitter whenever she can. She's a dangerous, dour creature. You, of all people, should know the dangers of having a mother like that." His voice grows shriller. "The beautiful light my little girl carries terrifies that woman. If Moira stays with Selkie, it could kill her. It will break her spirit, at minimum." He storms toward his truck. "But you do as you must!"

CHAPTER 7
MAD HOUSE OF PLAID

I tell myself that I misheard Clancy, that he didn't just speak the phrase that was written in blood on Mom's chest, that he didn't mock Lara's investigative powers because she rightly suspects him of killing my mother. But I can't deny my concerns. I need to speak to Police Chief Lara Oakley, right away.

En route, I pass Selkie's house, with its white exterior and Kelly-green shamrock shutters. Unlike that quaint exterior, the inside looks like an Irish insane asylum forever decorated for the Christmas holidays. I hate the idea of stopping but I need to update her on my conversation with her husband, no matter how difficult that may be. She has the right to know what her scumbag-of-a-man is up to.

I knock on the open door and her Abyssinian cat, Aisling, pushes it from the other side. The smell of Eau de Febreeze, unchanged cat litter, dirty dishes, overdue garbage, and stale laundry instantly hits me. Aisling greets me with a distrustful blink of her blinding golden eyes. Selkie runs up and snatches the cat. I cautiously step into this vomitous riot of endless red and green tartans.

"Thank God you've come!" Selkie cries, spewing vodka breath. Her long hair is not its usual silky well-brushed golden brown streaked with gray. It's a teased-up rat's nest from hell.

"I've called everyone else." She shakes me. "Please tell me Moira is with you! Please say you've heard from her! Say something, Snowy! Anything!"

"What are you talking about? I have no idea where Moira is," I plead.

Selkie slaps my cheek. "You're lying!"

"Ow!" I grab my sore cheek. "What's happened?"

Selkie tears at her hair, ratting it into more knots. "I went to My-stick River Day Camp to pick up Moira, and there was no sign of her."

My soul drains out onto the red and green plaid carpet. I realize I need to fess up fast because Clancy just stole their kid.

I choke out my words. "Clancy stopped by my place. I didn't see Moira with him. But she might have been inside his truck. I can't say for sure."

Selkie spits at me. She curses my female reproductive parts and my immortal soul. Ugly questions spill out of her throat, including why in hell her husband would visit my house unless I'm sleeping with him, like everyone else. I explain that I had no advance warning about his visit, and that NO, I'm not sleeping with my uncle. I bite my tongue and stop myself from saying I would never sleep with my mom's leftovers.

We hop in her Chevy Spark and ignore every red light en route to the Mystick Police station. Officer Mary Burd is stationed at the front desk. She tries to slip into the bathroom when she sees me coming.

"We have an emergency to report," I say, stopping her. "This woman's daughter is missing."

Mary whistles between two fingers. "Hold it right there, Strangeways. The child has probably gone off with her dad. The fact that the excursion is unapproved by her mom may be irritating, but it's not criminal. I may be mistaken but I believe the kid's parents remain married." Mary turns to Selkie, "Are you divorced Mrs. O'Connor?"

"Never," she says.

"Just as I thought," Mary notes. "You are a woman of faith." She pauses and shoots me a look that says, "you on the other hand, are a heathen ho."

"Selkie," says Mary, "I often see you at mass at Our Lady of the River. Keep the faith. I'll bet Clancy took Moira to the Silver Scoop Ice Cream Parlor. After the big mother-daughter argument you had this morning, I'm not surprised. I'm sure they'll be home, soon enough."

I whisper to Selkie, "What argument?"

She whispers back, "It was a small disagreement. Our nosy neighbors phoned the cops."

This new development makes me hope Moira is with Clancy. I'd hate to think Selkie scared the girl away, caused her some injury, or worse. In either case, I need to get the cops stirred up enough to search for Moira, just in case. A bold idea pops into my head. It may bring terrible trouble to an old family friend but at least it will impel the police into action. Besides, what if that dear old family friend really is the child catcher that half this town claims him to be?

I slam my palm onto the reception desk. "Clancy visited me at my house this morning."

Mary leers at my short lemon skirt and metallic gold stilettos. "That doesn't surprise me."

"Let's stick to the case, Hairy T." I say, holding her gaze. "Clancy mentioned something about Moira visiting Riley Finch."

"That makes no sense," she dismisses. "Clancy is smart enough to keep his kid away from that man."

"Since when is Clancy O'Connor the sharpest pencil in the box?" I ask.

Mary draws air between her teeth. "Fair enough."

She starts making calls. Despite Riley's temporary reprieve as Slaney's barge captain, nobody fully trusts a guy who was found with a young girl locked in his shed.

Selkie whispers in my ear. "Why did you lie to that cop? You know Clancy would never let Moira visit Riley."

"It's the only way I could convince him to get busy looking for her."

Selkie hugs my arm.

Police sirens sound in seconds.

We return to Selkie's place. I stick around to ensure there's a sober grown up in the house to greet her, if she comes home. We watch a movie on The Lifetime Channel about some guy who's cheating on his three wives. A knock on the door breaks the tension in the room. I dash to answer it. A stone-faced cop steps inside. Selkie starts sobbing.

The officer rushes to her aide, "No, ma'am. I don't have any bad news." She slouches, relieved, and he continues, "We just want you to know we brought Riley Finch in for questioning. He admitted to seeing Moira today. He said he was working at the seaport when she hopped a Boston Whaler with someone. Riley thinks it was a woman. He's not sure if there was a man with them. It was too foggy to see."

Selkie runs to her bedroom, wailing, "I knew it. Clancy found a new mom for Moira!"

I pull the officer aside and whisper. "Listen, Clancy told me he has a new girlfriend. She might be the woman Riley saw. Can I have a word with Police Chief Lara Oakley?

"I'm sorry but that's not possible," he says. "Chief Oakley has left town."

CHAPTER 8
SNOWLY

I shout over the racket of whatever bash Fríða's hosting. "I'm in The City. After I get my roots done, can we grab lunch?"

"I have pressing legal matters to attend to," she hollers back into the phone.

"That's what the noise is all about? Your legal matters? You're ghosting me," I conclude.

"I'm not the one who ran away and lost my Víðsýni, living in that small-minded town full of kidnappers and murderers."

I grind my molars. "Moira's only been gone two days. The police already have a lead on her case."

"Only two days? Do you hear yourself, Snowy? It's lucky you don't have children of your own, if you can act so casual about a kid who's been missing for two days."

"*Work pays the bills. Worry only kills.*"

"So now you're quoting me! What are you working on?"

"Granite House, for Lyr Corby."

Fríða doesn't respond. The hullabaloo at her end turns fractious, more like a political meeting than a party. Then the background noise abruptly fades, like she's stepped into a hallway or bathroom. "Don't use Perrini for that one. She won't do a job for Corby."

"Why not?"

Fríða groans, "A million reasons. Anyway, I have another fabricator. Go to the white stone building on Admiral's Row at the old Brooklyn Naval Yard. Ring the buzzer at the rolling gate. They'll be expecting you. Good luck." She hangs up without saying goodbye.

I arrive at a building that is crumbling like an ancient ruin.

A thicket of saplings has erupted from its roofless center, leaving a single corner room still intact and unexposed to the elements. The phrase "Run while you still can!" is painted in a cartoon word balloon above its entryway.

Someone taps my shoulder from behind, and I jump.

"I'm Ivor," says a scratchy whisper of a human with a hit man's face. He's wearing a wife beater and a pair of pants with ragged hems.

"I'm Snow-y," I say, over-pronouncing the end of my name.

He removes the mangled toothpick from between his teeth and uses it to point at a tall woman with an ill-fitting black shag wig and bad posture who's wearing a cheap fishnet dress. "Snowly, this is Zura."

Zura narrows her eyes at me in greeting. I try to return the bizarre look.

Ivor scans the street to make sure no one is watching before he unlocks the door and waves us inside.

Zura nudges me through the door, toward a beat up diner style table and says, "No worries. Any friend of Fríða is a friend of ours."

"Likewise," I say, wishing I meant it.

I try but fail to fully wipe off my seat with a tissue from my purse before sitting.

"Snowly. You want it, we make it." Ivor pats his narrow chest and coughs like he may have bronchitis or maybe emphysema or worse.

Zura and I both reach for a tissue to offer him. She pats down my hand, suggesting this is normal.

.   I pull away, in case he's contagious. "I wish to clarify that my name is Snowy," I state.

"Yes. Snowly," the both repeat.

My nostrils flair. "Can you please tell me what other projects you've done for Fríða?"

"This and that," shrugs Zura.

Ivor makes murderous eyes at her. She returns the expression.

He sticks out his lower lip, "You should no be fussy when job is for Lyr Corby."

"Lyr is unpopular?"

Zura widens her golf ball eyes at me. "She's dangerous."

Ivor pounds his tiny chest. "We only do this job as favor to Fríða because she look after us." He tosses his small chin into the air. "She help everybody. She protect us from narrow-minded people."

I put my hand to my heart. "I get it. I'm not like most people, either. Fríða also did a lot for me, growing up."

Zura and Ivor survey me, up and down, from my stilettos to my white hair. They stick out their lower lips, as if impressed. Zura relaxes a little. But remains distant. I hand her the sketches with specs for what I need.

"Can you make these furnishings and fixtures?" I ask.

Ivor clucks, which I suppose is a good thing.

I'm thumbing through my purse for a checkbook when he waves his hands across his chest.

"No money," he says. "We owe much to Fríða. We make what you want by end of week."

Zura stares at me as if she is still waiting for something. It's not money. A sign, maybe? I notice her gray roots and take a shot in the dark.

"May the blessings of the goddesses Arianhrod, Cerridwen, and Macha be with you always," I say.

She holds her hands to her heart. "May the goddesses shine on you, as well," she lauds.

Zura gives Ivor an "I told you so" look.

CHAPTER 9
MYSTICK PICNICK

I collapse on my faded blue sailcloth sofa, starved from my whirlwind trip to The City. I order a garlic and clam pizza and drift into a dream. In it, I'm replacing the old mermaid sign out front with a new aluminum steel one shaped like an abstract wave, when I'm wakened by the rapping sound of Slaney's Danish mermaid door-knocker.

I hop up, excited to greet the pizza delivery dude. But behind my door stands a gray-haired woman with an Upper West Side ponytail, cradling a pot of blue pin-striped geraniums. Her skin stretches across her face as if she's facing a perpetual high wind. I recognize her; it's Zola Black. She's the woman I saw with Alse at Slaney's funeral.

I've seen Zola Black's face on dozens of magazine covers, usually wearing something inspired by an exotic plant or animal. Today, she's dressed simply, in an oversized man's shirt, torn jeans and running shoes—an outfit that screams "moving clothes." I can't make a single drop of conversation flow from my brain to my lips.

"Greetings, lovely, I'm Zola Black," she announces in that sing song voice of hers.

Her dolphin gray eyes dissect my home interiors, halting when they reach Slaney's self-portrait. She speaks to me while staring at it. "What an honor to meet the young design prodigy herself: the illusive Snowy Strangeways." She moves her gaze from the portrait to the room furnishings and catches her breath when she spots the plain white cotton window sashes. Our hands brush in a cool handshake, and she recovers her focused game face.

"Having a Manhattan design star like you for my new country neighbor was quite a selling point for me, Snowy. I felt sure I wouldn't need to worry about inflatable Christmas decorations popping up next door, if you know what I mean," She beams and shoves a pot of pin-striped geraniums at my chest. "These are for you. I can't grow a thing. I'm not much of a nurturer, despite my famous plant and animal designs."

I examine the odd flowers. "These don't look very natural."

"They're not. Some sort of new hybrid. They're the official geraniums of the Bronx.

"Are you a Yankees fan?" I ask, incredulous.

"I was," she sighs, "until Alex Rodriguez retired. Those magnificent green eyes!"

I pat my flower pot, not interested in discussing has-been baseball players.

A downy auburn kitten pokes out of Zola's oversized shirt pocket.

I nearly drop my geraniums.

"See what I mean about my lack of nurturing?" She giggles. "I almost forgot to feed my baby. This is Russ. He's a ruddy Somali. You can't yet get a true sense of his mature coloring. He'll assume his full russet glory soon." Zola's eyes glisten, "Wait till you see him at his best, Lovely. He's a designer's delight!"

I place the geraniums outside my front door. The angel inside my head wants to complement Zola on her stunning geraniums, cute kitty, and illustrious career, but the pitchfork-toting varmint in my head wins out as usual.

"What really brings you to our fair town?" I ask.

Russ meows and I force myself to pet him with my pinky.

Her face stiffens, as if searching for her publicist's talking points on this subject. She readily brightens, as if remembering her lines. "I've spent so much time traveling that I've never decorated an entire house for myself. I thought it was time for me to find an old home by the sea and settle down. I'm getting along and need to leave a legacy. I want the house next door to be my Magnus opus, reflecting the best of humanity."

I gulp back the word, "bullshit," and add some of my own, "I look forward to the privilege of having a front row seat as your glorious eco-designs blossom next door."

"Not at all!" Zola bursts out, like I've poked one of her inner demons. "I no longer derive design inspiration from natural plants and animals. I've entered a new phase, or rather, returned to an old one." She pats Russ's head. In design school, we had a professor who made us study Michelangelo." She shakes her fists. "Oh, how we loathed her! Although, I now see where she was going by teaching us his work. The man's use of color and symbolism was divine. I love that he created three sculptures of the pieta, three sections in the Sistine Chapel, three frescoes of God. I feel so guilty about the wicked names your grandmother and I called that poor teacher, back in the day."

"You knew Slaney in design school?" I gulp.

She wipes away a single tear. "You didn't know that? I'm surprised she never mentioned me. We attended Parsons together in The City. We were both sixteen when we started, just like you. We were also foolish. Freshman year, I wound up in handcuffs for sneaking into the Bronx Zoo to get close to the langurs, and your grandmother got pregnant with Selkie while she was studying abroad."

"Did you meet my grandfather, back then?"

"That was years later. Slaney and I were visiting the museum on the Mohegan Reservation, seeking design inspiration. Your grandmother found that inspiration when she met him. I was devastated that he ignored me." She reaches over and squeezes my hand. "I went through a rough time after that and made some bad mistakes."

"I'm sorry to hear that," I say. "Please tell me more about my grandfather."

She waves her palm at the door. "May I come inside, first?"

"Of course," I blush, and usher her inside.

My purse and shoes are strewn across the sofa. So Zola sits in the Nantucket red armchair that faces the glass coffee table, set with a bowl of seashells. She waves her hand over the shells, as if hoping to erase them. I'm glad she can't see the master bedroom's tacky brass porthole windows and stucco-ed blue-gray walls from where she sits.

I shove my things off the sofa and flop onto it.

She folds her hands under her well-nipped and tucked chin. "Back to your grandfather. He and Slaney were in love. Things worked out well, for a while. In the end, their relationship could not survive their cultural divide."

I sit up rod straight. "Their cultural divide?" Photographs of gorgeous Maori, Cape Verdean, Romani, and Uyghur men run through my mind. "What country was my grandfather from?"

"What country?" She tosses back her head, laughing; in that sarcastic Gray posture I've seen a million times. "Lovely, your grandfather is the only person I ever met who truly came from right here." She points a finger at the floor. "He was a Mohegan Indian."

I shake my head, disbelieving. "If my grandfather is Mohegan, that would make me a Native American."

She strains her long neck my way. "You didn't know?"

"I feel a hot rush, recalling the way Supreme Gray Wolf Gertie Mazeen was always eager to share tribal traditions with me and was the only one who ever listened to me about my visions."

"With your looks, Snowy, I find it odd you never guessed you possess Native American ancestry."

"Nope. I was clueless," I fume. "What was my grandfather's name?"

"We called him Wolfie."

"Wolfie?" My mind speeds through everything Gertie ever told me about her tribe, my tribe. "Mohegan means 'wolf people.' Wolfie could refer to any Mohegan."

Zola's eyes roam the inside of Mermaid Cottage. They twitch at the dried starfish in the windows. "Slaney's loss of Wolfie and Rebekah clearly took a toll on the quality of her design work." She pounds the coffee table top and the shells jump. "Speaking of style, I was telling you about Michelangelo's theories and how I now see the genius in his work."

"What do you find most impressive about him?" I say, pretending to care.

"His humanism," she stipulates. "Good interior designs always reflects humanism's best qualities. Have you seen the Sistine Chapel?" She throws out two open palms as if considering that Italian masterpiece, at this very moment.

I stare blankly. The Sistine Chapel is cave art to me. But I don't say that because it hits me that the world's greatest designer is seated in my living room.

I force out my real concern. "Are you planning to open a design studio, next door?"

She examines her nails which are coated reflectively, like mirrors. "Yes, I plan to use the house as a showcase for my new rooms."

I'm proud of myself for not screaming. I find strength and comfort in knowing my grandma never lived to see this day. I stare at her well-worn chestnut floorboards and say, "It sounds like I'm about to become a tacky Canal Street knock-off, camped out in your Madison Avenue gutter."

"Certainly not. You're a world-class designer." She lowers her voice, "Although I did hear an ugly rumor that you're working for that Corby woman. Do be warned. She has a bad reputation for running out on bill collectors."

I'm about to ask her why I should care, considering she's out to destroy my family business, when something registers as suspicious. "Who told you I'm working for Lyr?"

Zola flicks a reflective fingernail at the coffee table. "Busted! I had scones and seaweed tea this morning with Alse Critchley at The Silver Moon. The waitress leaked that you grabbed a bite at the crack of dawn, on your way to The City to source materials for Granite House." She forms triangular and diamond shapes with her fingers. "I love how their scones form unusual shapes. Don't you?"

I narrow my eyes.

"I have something for you," says Zola.

She hands me a card, and my heart falls out of my chest.

VIP EARLY ENTRY
ZB Interior Design Showcase
Come View "Mystick Picnick"
This Saturday 10 AM
2713 River Road, Mystick, CT
Free Chowders & Local Brews

"You're showcasing a room already? You're offering free beer and chowder? The whole town will be there." I recheck the invitation. "There's no way you can be ready by Saturday. No one has started working on Mons…your house."

She chuckles deep within her chest. "It's only one room, Lovely. My people can install it in a wink. Do come see it. I value your professional opinion."

My face falls when I realize I should be pressing the search for my missing cousin, not viewing the competition's design showcase.

Zola places her hand on mine. "I'm so sorry. I forgot that you have more important things on your mind. Alse told me the horrible news about little Moira O'Connor going missing. That's hardly the sort of thing I expected to hear happening in a quaint little town like Mystick."

I feel my lower lip quiver and hope she doesn't notice. "Mystick's small town police force is the problem."

Zola thunders back. "My thoughts exactly! Alse told me they never solved your Mom's murder. I can't believe it. Not a single arrest in eight years. That's absurd."

My mind takes a tally of Zola's actions. First, she reveals bombshell family information about my grandfather being a Mohegan, named Wolfie. Then she discloses disturbing news about Lyr's tardy bill paying. She discusses scone shapes because she knows I love geometry. Then she mentions Moira's kidnapping and Mom's murder. She is an expert on my pain, past and present. My head is spinning. But I don't fear a vision coming on. Snooping into people's home interiors is the last thing on my mind.

"Snowy," she wraps a warm arm around me. "I know a brilliant New York detective named Manny Spellman. I took the liberty of contacting him. He's willing to investigate Moira's case. I'd be happy to fund his services. It's the least I can do, considering I've descended upon your family's design territory, unbidden."

I can't speak.

She continues, "Manny could also look into your mom's case. Wouldn't you like a fresh set of eyes on that old burning question?"

I feel a surge of gratitude. "I'd love it," I blather.

"Then, it's settled. He'll be here tomorrow." She jots down his phone number with a Sharpie on one of her transparent Lucite business cards.

I look to Slaney's portrait of a woman inside a glass box, trapped underwater. I picture Mom's painting at Granite house of a boxed-in head. Slaney managed to survive the glass box of her small home and small business in a small town. Mom did not. Have I inherited Mom's crushing head box? Slaney's stifling house box? Am I creating a new box of my own?

I stop Zola with a hand at the door. "Despite your desire to open a design studio next door, I won't let anything happen to Slaney Strangeways, Decorating. I hope you understand that."

She sets her hands on my shoulders. "Actually, I'm hoping you'll consider an alternative, that Slaney would appreciate. Snowy Strangeways, would you partner with me at my new design studio, next door?"

CHAPTER 10
MANNY ON THE CASE

The Manhattan train screeches into the Mystick station. Passengers hop off, choking on laughter, ready to frolic in the countryside—all except the giant with the silver goatee and shaved head who bursts out of the last car. He's slugging a Day-Glo orange can of some energy drink I don't recognize. Two more bright drink cans fill the oversized pockets of his long gray gabardine duster. His monstrous pewter boots buckle, tie, and knot, with superhero complexity. The top of his chest bulges enough to support a load of wood. I presume it's his buzz drink habit that makes the bones in his face appear so razor sharp.

He flinches when our eyes meet, and then points at me with both index fingers, like a stickup artist. "Hey there, kid." He extends a hand. "Manny Spellman. You're my contact, right?"

His Mad Max-Wild West demeanor make me nod, fast, like a two-year-old. "Yes," I point to myself, "I'm Snowy Strangeways."

"Snowy. Love the name. Not the one you were born with. Am I right?" Those two fingers pop up again.

I giggle like I'm four and follow him to a black Mercedes that Zola rented for him. I think how Slaney never owned a car. It's a big Gray Goddess no-no. But I might like to own one. Stilettos and long walks don't mix. This thought brings me back to contemplating Zola's offer.

"To the batmobile?" Manny says, noticing that I've zoned out.

"Right," I say, giggling harder.

How does he know I'm a closet batman fan? I can't help it; the idea of a superhero with a super-stylish lair is irresistible to me.

He nails the gas. I grip the door handle the whole way down

River Road. We squeal into Selkie's driveway. She's waiting at the door, pupils cloudy with meds and booze. At first sight of Manny, she yanks him inside. The place smells worse than usual, like despair has its own peculiarly vile stench.

"Easy now," he cautions, taking a seat in the oak rocker Slaney bought as a nursing chair, a chair that I doubt Selkie ever used. I picture her dumping icy bottles of lumpy baby formula down Moira's throat, when she bothered to feed her at all.

Aisling is clawing at the plaid draperies. I wish she'd keep clawing until every bit of plaid fabric in this place is destroyed. I know that Selkie went along with Clancy's tartan obsession because it kept Slaney from visiting their home. Colorful patterned interiors made Slaney physically ill. The Gray Goddesses generally enjoy understated designs. I take a seat on a plain red footstool that's the only non-plaid piece of furniture.

Selkie dumps a pile of photos on Manny's lap. "These pictures show Moira's favorite hangouts—the Silver Scoop Ice Cream Parlor, Mystick River Day Camp, Mystick Aquarium, and Mystick Seaport." She grits her teeth. "Her father took these pictures." She hands Manny a piece of rumpled yellow legal paper. "Here's a list of the girl's vitals: weight, height, hair and eye color. There's a cat's paw birthmark on her right shoulder. Such a perfect little Gray, that child."

Manny rises. "Thanks, Mrs. O'Connor. Gonna find your daughter." He touches her hair and then pulls back.

The second Manny exits, she beelines for a pill bottle on the kitchen counter.

"You need to stay sober in case Moira comes home," I remind her.

She holds up a single pill and swallows it, to show me she's not over-medicating.

"I'm still staying here because I don't trust you," I warn.

She yawns and heads for her bedroom.

I sit on a green plaid kitchen counter stool and try to sketch designs for the dreaded Granite House kitchen. Fríða has made it clear she's not helping me design anything for Lyr.

Three hours later, all I've come up with is a sketch of a chair design for the breakfast nook. The backs are shaped like a letter L—for loser. It's clear I'm distracted by Zola's offer. If I'm good enough to be her partner, aren't I good enough to be her competition?

The doorbell rings around four pm. Selkie runs to answer it with crossed eyes.

Manny appears, stooped and pale. "Found Moira's shoe," he huffs.

I throw my hands over my mouth.

Selkie gasps. "Was there blood on it?"

Manny and I exchange hard glances. Aisling swipes a scolding paw at Selkie.

"What kind of question is that, Selkie?" I ask.

"No blood," Manny injects. "Police have it. Matches the shoes in a photo you gave me."

"Moira's father wouldn't let her lose a shoe. A stranger must have taken her." Selkie snivels.

"Don't be so sure." Manny brushes back her long silky hair.

Selkie tugs on his shirt. "Why?"

Manny tosses me a troubled glance. "Found it near the last known location of the Prakesh kid."

"What? Who?" I burst out.

He bites his lip. "Nahla's also missing." He pulls out her soccer team photo and points to her intense olive-colored eyes. "Two stand-out kids. Should be easy to spot."

"Exactly. From what I hear, Lucy Wauby—the Pequot girl who was kidnapped eight years ago— was also stunning."

For the first time I feel grateful that my plain looks, as a kid.

Selkie's face turns wild. "Nahla is Moira's best friend. What can this mean? Is Nahla's mom out of rehab? Does she know her daughter is missing?"

Manny shakes his head no. "Nahla's Mom is still in treatment." He eyes Selkie with soft distant eyes, as if she reminds him of an old flame. "Anyway, two missing girls may be better than one."

"Better!" I want to smack him, until I figure out what he means. "Wait…You think Clancy nabbed both Nahla and Moira."

Manny frowns. "Yep. Maybe Moira got bored. Maybe Clancy

grabbed her best friend. Kid saw her, got excited, and pitched a shoe."

Selkie claps her hands together. "Then she's fine. My little girl is fine."

I lower my eyes. Manny's theory is pretty far-fetched. What if Clancy is not involved in either kidnapping? What if he is living in Ireland without Moira, enjoying a frothy Guinness and crispy fish and chips with his new sugar mama? In that case, a lost shoe suggests Moira's kidnapper is a child serial killer. But I keep this theory to myself, for the time being.

"Snowy, need your help with some follow-up work," says Manny. "Grab a bite?"

"I'll come, too," proposes Selkie, staggering toward Manny.

He steadies her. "Wait here, in case Moira calls."

"Right," she sneers.

Manny and I stroll down Main Street towards the drawbridge. I can't help checking out every red-haired kid on the street.

A man huddled under a large bent piece of cardboard holds out a tin can that says "Anything—Please." All I can see of his face are two bloodshot eyes. I've never seen anyone panhandling in downtown Mystick. The Grays keep the local homeless shelter and soup kitchen well-funded, to avoid tarnishing the town's sweet little old lady image. Could this guy be a poser? Or worse, what if he's Moira's kidnapper? Manny leans down to drop some change into the man's can. Panhandlers don't freak him out because he's from The City. They don't usually freak me out, either. But something about this particular homeless man makes my skin tingle like a fresh wound.

The man extends a bony arm out from under the cardboard and snatches Manny's ankle. "Good -o see you, sir."

I notice he doesn't pronounce his "t's" and experience a flash of recognition. He sounds like the same man who was yelling *Doo-was yoo-mas - Do as you must* from the roof of the Silver Moon, the day of Slaney's funeral. The man's eyes connect with mine. He jumps up and dashes away, the dirty tails of his long gray coat trailing behind him.

I lunge to follow him but Manny dives to pull me back. "Whoa!" he says.

"I know that guy," I try to shake free. "He's pretending to be homeless."

Manny's voice turns gruff. "Nah, straight-up down and out. Doesn't need more trouble." His face turns reproachful.

My lips tremble. "He might be my mom's killer."

"That guy ain't no killer." Manny scratches his shaved head. "You got some kind of PTSD?"

I huff, pulling away. "Possibly. But that doesn't change the fact that he's the same man I heard yelling the words written on my dead mom's chest."

"What words?"

"Do as you must."

He turns his back on me and paces. "Not much of a clue. Maybe lyrics from a song." He starts humming. "Wait a minute." He snaps his finger in the air. "Got it! David Thomas! Came out before you were born. You wouldn't know it." He sings, "*Say what you will and do as you must. Deeds are alive when the man turns to dust.*"

"I'm not convinced. But I'll drop it . . . for now," I grunt.

We walk into the Silver Moon. Alse leers at Manny from across the room. We choose seats at a table as far away from her as possible. She stoops over, letting the ends of her long iron hair dangle into her cup of seaweed tea. Her hand squeezes her infamous cane for support. The restorative energy of Slaney's funeral has clearly worn off. Alse is back to her old dilapidated self. The Grays need to make a speedy decision about Slaney's successor. Alse won't be able to carry on as Acting Supreme Gray Goddess for much longer.

I point to the portrait that sits over the fireplace. "That's Mystick's first Supreme Gray Goddess, Rebekah Wright. Moira is also destined to become Mystick's Supreme Gray Goddess, one day," I explain to Manny.

Manny throws shade at Alse. "Let's make sure she's around to do that."

He orders an espresso before I have the chance to warn him that it won't be strong enough. I order a seaweed tea because Grandma Slaney said this swampy brew connects Grays to the power of the sea, and I need all the help I can get.

Alse observes me sipping seaweed tea and taps her fingers on her palm, applauding. Manny shoots her the kind of look that cops give to cop killers. She harrumphs at him, pulls herself up to a standing position and limps out the door, teetering on her cane.

"What was that all about?" I ask.

He growls out the words, "That old broad took a man's eye and walked. Don't want her cane near me."

"Fair enough," I say, holding up two shaking hands. "But there's something more going on here."

He rubs his hand over his shaved head. "You're right. Had to clear the room. Nobody else can see this." He scans the room and whips out a crumpled three by five-inch photograph. It shows Police Chief Lara Oakley kissing Clancy O'Connor.

"No way!" My loud exclamation draws the waitress's eye, and I lower my voice. "Now I see why you needed to speak to me, apart from Selkie. Where did you get this trashy photo?"

"Stole it from Lara Oakley's desk drawer."

"You stole a photograph from the Mystick Police Chief. How?"

"Donut patrol was watching videos. Just snuck in and grabbed it."

"She'll notice it's gone."

"Sure. Might put her on edge. Push her to make a mistake. Give herself away."

"You're a boss at this detective stuff."

"Yeah, I know."

"I get that Lara Oakley isn't pursuing leads on Moira's kidnapping because she's in on it with Clancy. But what if their love affair isn't new? What if they've been seeing one another on and off for years? I wouldn't put it past Clancy to have been doing both Mom and Lara at the same time." I grab my gut. This sick thought on top of the seaweed tea mixed makes me push away my mug.

Manny also grimaces. "Lara ever question Clancy about your mom's murder?"

"She claimed she found no concrete evidence against him."

"Convenient." He leans back and flexes his fists. "Think Lara murdered your mom? Keep Rebekah away from her boyfriend, maybe?"

"Possibly. Do you think Clancy was in on it?"

"Doubtful. More of a lover than a killer." Manny slams his palm on the table, knocking the gooey contents of a ceramic honey pot onto the hand-woven tablecloth. "Sorry." He tries to clean up the sticky mess with a daisy napkin. "Riley saw Moira with a woman, right?"

"Yes, that's right," I nod.

He frowns. "Had to be Lara. Nobody questions a cop picking up a kid. Riley left out mentioning her name because of his outstanding kidnapping issue. Riley rats Lara out, she arrests him. His freedom is her security, and vice versa."

Thunderheads roll down the river. The café darkens. Manny hasn't touched his espresso. I've hardly touched my tea.

Our Gray waitress brings wet towels to clean up the honey mess and asks, "Are you finished with your drinks?"

"All yours," we say, in sync, shoving our still-full mugs her way.

I lean into Manny and whisper. "I'm guessing you lied to Selkie, when you told her the police know about Moira's shoe."

Manny points with both fingers. "You got me! Saw the photo and kept the shoe. Police Chief is our prime suspect, after all."

"How are we going to get the girls back, with the Chief of Police in on the kidnappings?"

"Here's the thing, Snowy. Selkie's kid's better off with her dad till we figure out our next move."

"Are you suggesting that we do nothing?"

"Temporarily. Meantime, let's look at your Mom's murder. We prove Lara did it, and we can call the feds. Grays won't like them snooping around and they'll let Lara take the fall."

I squirm. "How much do you know about the Grays?"

"Harmless eccentrics. Like most of New York City." His eyes sharpen. "Let's refocus on your mom. What happened the day she died?"

I turn my face toward the window and tear up. Summer tourists hustle into the downtown shops as light raindrops start to fall.

"Lara was the first cop to arrive at Mom's murder scene," I recount. "She was quick, getting there. Wait a minute. Maybe she was inside my house all along!"

Manny hits my shoulder with a dog-eared manila folder he's retrieved from a super-sized pocket in his coat. "Now you're thinking,

Sherlock. Lara's report says you stepped in Rebekah's blood." He hands me the folder. "And Snowy," he pauses, "she claims your blood was mingled with your mom's."

My mind drifts back to that gruesome crime scene. Words burst out of my mouth. "Barnacle bit me. That's why my blood was there."

"Who's Barnacle?"

"Slaney's cat."

He elbows me. "You got into a catfight at your mom's murder scene?"

I elbow him back. "You don't know Barnacle. Anyway, when Lara arrived, she took me upstairs and removed my running shoes. Then she put me to bed until the ambulance arrived." I grab his arm. "I'll bet the bitch framed me with those sneakers." I throw back my head. "I thought she was just incompetent. She's actually pretty tricky. Tell me Manny: how do you take down a bad small town cop?"

Manny stands up to his full height of nearly seven feet. "With two bad ass New Yorkers," he says. "Let's put Lara behind bars, blow this town, and get back to civilization."

He holds the door for me to exit the Silver Moon. I hesitate. "I'm not sure I'll be returning to New York. Zola Black offered me a partnership in her new Mystick design studio."

His arms widen to embrace the universe. "ZB wants Snowy Strangeways! Don't look so glum. That's bigtime, kid. Huge." He hugs me.

A familiar voice shouts from behind us on the sidewalk, "Hey Snowy! Aren't you going to introduce me to your friend?"

I roll my eyes. I stupidly forgot that *Mystick Lights'* newspaper office is right next door to the Silver Moon. Kai's journalist's nose twitches at Manny. I need a phony cover story, fast. I don't want Kai letting our town's corrupt police department find out what Manny and I know.

I step between the two men. Kai's my height, which is tall for normal humans but still a head shorter than Manny. "Hi Kai. This is my new client, Manny Spellman."

I give Manny a play-nice look, and say, "Mr. Spellman, this is my 'Perhaps Friend,' Kai Corby. He works for *Mystick Lights* newspaper."

"A Perhaps Friend?" Manny winks at Kai. "Or Perhaps More?"

Kai death-glares Manny. "None of your business, dude. Where are you from? Something tells me it's not Mystick." Sweat glistens on his brow, or maybe it's the misting rain.

Manny hitches his shoulders. "You got me. I'm a New Yorker. Buying a shoreline home. Wanna get out of The City. Live the good life. A friend recommended Ms. Strangeways for the interiors. She's terrific." He pats Kai on the back. "Need to catch a train. Gotta go, son." Manny packs himself into his rental car.

"Son, my ass!" Kai shouts as Manny drives away. His eyes follow the car until it's out of sight. "That guy acts like he jumped out of a Sam Spade novel."

I step away from Kai. "Mr. Copper Pen makes fun of someone because they're old fashioned?"

"He's obviously a private dick, not to mention a public one."

"Fine, he's a dick but only in the professional sense of the word. You need to dive beneath the surface, once in a while. Take Armando, the bouncer we had at Hips."

"The strip club where you were raised?" His face contorts.

"Exactly. He's the scariest human I've ever seen. His arms bulge like twisted tree roots and his face resembles a melted scrap metal heap. But when I was eleven, he built me an amazing dollhouse so I could practice designing room interiors. That dollhouse let me make mistakes on the cheap. Sure, Armando looked like a supervillain. But he was generous and nurturing. Appearances mean nothing."

"Forget the speech, Snowy," rejects Kai. "I also grew up with the Grays. Remember? They're far from the sweet little old ladies they pretend to be. I know all about phony appearances. And that guy is hiding something." He shakes a finger in my direction.

All the air rushes out of me. "Zola hired him to find Moira. He's also helping me find out who killed my mom."

He punches the air. "Okay, thank you for that one piece of the truth. But why would a guy from The City take a small-town detective job in Mystick unless there's some bigger hook? Maybe he wants to make Lara Oakley look bad so he can replace her and take her job. Detectives often hold cop credentials. I'll bet Zola's told all her big city friends that we're easy marks in this small town. Manny is job shopping for Lara Oakley's Chief of Police position. She's an easy mark."

"Paranoid much?" I jeer.

"Look at the facts, Snowy. First, Zola moves in next door to intimidate you, so you won't bother trying to sell Slaney's decorating business. Then—just to be sure you don't update it and compete with her—she offers to hire you to work with her."

"How did you find out that Zola offered me a job?"

He leers. "I didn't. It was a lucky guess."

"I still plan to sell Slaney's business."

"Then why haven't I seen a 'For Sale' sign go up yet?"

My mind races through possible answers to that question. I pick the most convincing one. "Moira's kidnapping distracted me."

"Working with Manny on your mom's case will also keep you distracted. Zola knows that. She didn't become rich and famous by not thinking ahead. Mark my words, she'll manipulate you into working for her. She's already made the head of local law enforcement look bad by paying Manny to investigate her highest profile criminal cases. The next thing you know, some retired *New York Times* editor friend of hers will buy *Mystick Lights* from Alse and replace Nori Moon. Then more of Zola's Manhattan friends will swoop in to claim our remaining small town jobs. And presto, we've lost our town. Be careful, Snowy. You may not love Mystick. But do you want to be responsible for destroying it?"

"I'm not sure I care. Nori is a bottom feeder. Lara's a bumpkin whose skills don't hack it for solving major crimes. I won't protect the jobs of Mystick losers from qualified New Yorkers."

His eyes grow hard. "You're not giving this town a fair chance because you blame it for killing your mom."

My bottom lip trembles. "I also blame it for allowing Moira O'Connor and Nahla Prakesh to get kidnapped." My eyes follow the line of Kai's nose scar. "You claim Manny is sketchy. You just dumped your fiancé. I'll bet you got that nose scar in a bar fight. Your mom hides out in a secret stone fortress on a hill. Nobody knows exactly what she does for a living. Plus, the New York design community says she doesn't pay her bills."

I withdraw an envelope from my purse and hand it to Kai. "I'm no small-town toady. My work is top shelf. She may not be able to afford me. See to it that she receives this bill for my design services so there are no misunderstandings."

CHAPTER 11
MICHELANGELO

The misty morning air crackles with electricity. Mysticks queue up for Zola's new room showcase in a line that stretches from her house into my holly bushes. According to Slaney's Irish superstitions, holly bushes protect against bad spirits. I'm glad for that protection today because the Grays are out in gale force to support their glittering new idol, never mind claim their free beer and chowder.

I can't deny that Zola oozes charm. Take her paint mixing ritual— which I've been forced to observe from my kitchen window for the last few days. She combines tints and base colors: stirring, turning her head to catch the sunlight, shaking it nay or yay, adjusting the hue, and then brushing and rebrushing the result onto a three by five board that she has leaned up against the trunk of the copper beech tree located between our houses. The old Zola would have designed an entire room based on the deep emerald and ruby colors of that tree. The new Zola shoots well past those sublime earthly hues, reaching for their cosmic counterparts of solar red and aurora borealis green. Like Michelangelo, she creates shades as brilliant as the first stellar rainbow that followed The Big Bang. This woman loves Michelangelo because she is Michelangelo.

A group of painters, wallpaper hangers, and carpenters exit Monster House, wiping their brows and tipping their sweaty baseball caps to the clapping crowd. Everything Zola planned appears to be moving forward, right on time, with the exception of my commitment to become her partner. Such an association would set me up for life. But a part of me still hopes that this design showcase will bomb, forcing her to close up shop and skip town.

Armed with the latest iridescent summer makeup, my VIP invitation, a cotton candy pink leather miniskirt, and a pair of clear strappy stiletto sandals, I strut past the gawking young wait staff, who try not to spill their trays of blueberry beer and clam chowder as I pass. I ring Zola's front doorbell, which plays a sea shanty sung by Mystick Seaport's favorite bard. Everyone in line claps when they hear it. I wink at the crowd, even though my heart is breaking. That Mystick sea shanty doorbell shows that Zola doesn't need me to schmooze the townies, which forces me to consider Kai's concerns about why she's offered me a partnership. Is her real ploy to eliminate Slaney Strangeways, Decorating? Is she still mad at Slaney for stealing Wolfie's affection?

Zola emerges from Monster House, wearing a white linen dress hand painted with a penguin, in homage to the ever-popular inhabitants of our local aquarium. Regardless of what she says about her new focus, she's still making an effort to please her animal-loving fans.

"Snowy Strangeways! Greetings, Lovely!" she glimmers. Her endless arms extend to pull me onto the front steps of The Monster. "Fellow Mysticks, we are honored to have such a tremendous local talent in attendance. You all knew the late great Slaney Strangeways. But some of you may not know her talented granddaughter, Snowy. This young woman has been honing her interior design skills at a top Manhattan design studio for the last few years. Gothamites call her a prodigy. As do I. Let's give a warm round of applause to Mystick's sublimely talented native daughter, Snowy Strangeways."

The Mysticks clap politely. A few whisper my real name. Others complain about my unnatural white hair color, the fact that my skirt is too short, that my heels are too high, and that my makeup is too heavy.

Zola wraps a tight arm around me and announces, "Lovelies, I want to become a positive part of this town. That means I need a true insider to guide me. Slaney Strangeways's talented granddaughter will fit the bill. Don't you think?"

Soft hissing follows.

I whisper to her, "Zola, I told you that I need time to consider your offer, and I mean it."

She strokes my hair. "You poor thing. You are underage. You can't hold a design license or handle contracts without an older designer covering for you. What other options do you have, now that Fríða is retiring and selling her interior design business?"

"What do you mean Fríða is retiring? She never mentioned that to me."

Her voice turns gritty. "Perhaps she was afraid you'd try and talk her out of retiring because you're angling to inherit Víðsýni."

My face grows hot. "Or maybe you told Fríða that you were offering me a partnership, and she assumed I'd jump at it and decided to throw in the towel."

"Either way, a partnership will benefit us both," Zola slides her tongue along her well-capped white teeth.

She pulls me to the microphone. "Snowy Strangeways, will you join me as a partner in my new design studio?"

Hoots and whistles fill the air.

Zola waves them into silence and turns to me. "Well?"

"I'm considering it," I say, with forced calm.

People look at me like I've suffered a traumatic head injury. But I know what I'm doing. Everybody in this town loved Slaney's work. Zola's local appeal is unknown. This showcase room could still bomb, and I refuse to bomb with it, by association.

"A tough fish to reel in!" winks Zola. Let's see if I can offer better bait."

I follow her inside The Monster. My legs are shaking but not because of her. This will be the first time I've set foot inside this house, where the kitchen was Mom's final design project. But I don't make it to the kitchen. I freeze the moment I hit the foyer. The spectacular entry chandelier Zola has installed nearly brings me to my knees. It's a jumble of wooden spikes and bulbs that conjures the image of an enchanted whaling ship. It should be featured in the Museum of Modern Art.

Zola stares at it, biting a fingernail painted like a celestial nebula, with pearl flakes glued here and there, to represent cosmic dust.

"Do you feel this chandelier speaks to the history of this town?" Zola murmurs. "Is it Mistickal enough?"

"It's dazzlingly appropriate," I confess.

She drums her fabulous fingers under her chin. "What is your impression of the flooring?"

My eyes turn to the transparent blue polymer coating she has laid over river rocks. This design winds down the hall, as if the Mystick River has decided to run indoors and out. .

"Also, dazzlingly appropriate," I reply.

I make my peace with the chandelier and hallway. But she can never truly appreciate the spirit of this quirky town. Capturing Mystick's weird whimsy will always be Slaney Strangeways's special domain.

One of her caterers pulls back a curtain on the room at the end of the hall. I shudder when I see its Mom's kitchen, still painted in the same outrageous green she chose before she died. Bile fills my mouth. This room looms before me like a deadly infection.

Zola pulls me into her featured new room. "Welcome to 'Mystick Picnick,'" she beckons.

I scan her design work and Slaney's legacy fades before me like river fog in the noonday sun.

The floor is laid with curved birch planks that form an abstract conch shell. A rectangular Lucite dining table base is painted with faint green lines, mimicking spiked leaves of grass. The top is tinted with translucent red and white squares, echoing a classic picnic tablecloth. Floor-to-ceiling natural linen curtains feature the faces of Mystick townsfolk picnicking by the drawbridge. Their toile-style images are printed in seaweed greens and crustacean reds. An abstract brass basket weave lighting fixture hangs over the table, completing the seaside picnic theme.

Zola wasn't kidding when she said her design philosophy had changed. This room is all about people enjoying nature for personal benefit, humans bending the environment to their will. The old Zola would have showcased Mystick's endangered eels, blueback herring, swamp birch, and milkweed. Her old designs inspired folks to send money to the World Wildlife Fund. This new room encourages people to stare into the mirror, admiringly, and then pat themselves on the back, merely for waking up as homo sapiens. Unlike the Mother Earth-loving style that made her famous, there's an air of human domination and entitlement to Zola's new work. Mystick Picnick makes people feel like they are frolicking Olympic gods, viewing planet earth from their omnipotent position among the clouds

The head caterer announces to the anxious crowd. "Ladies and gentlemen, Zola Black's new showcase room is now officially open. Please enter this way. We hope you enjoy this Mystick Picnick."

Cheers erupt as people crush through the front door of Monster House. Zola grabs the microphone and calls out, "Fellow Mysticks, I want to thank each of you for honoring me with your visit today. I want you to know how much this charming town has inspired me. Living and creating designs here has been a transformative experience. When you view this room, I hope you will agree that I needed this town to move my work to the next level. In fact, I was a failed designer, until now."

A chorus of "no's" fills the air. I groan. She's setting them up and playing them, like Murray does his bagpipes, like Clancy does his women.

Zola blushes right on queue. "For too long, I channeled the glorious images of plants and animals from faraway lands. But no more. My new source of inspiration is the people of this town." She opens her arms and draws them to her, in a gesture that reminds me of the one Alse made at Slaney's funeral.

A few people clap. Most exchange confused glances. Zola holds a frozen smile. I can smell her fear. Her new room is great but she did not advertise this shift in focus. Mysticks came here expecting to see a room designed by Mother Nature-loving Zola Black, not Michelangelo-loving Zola Black. The women who run this town call themselves Goddesses because they are proud lovers of the feminine divine. Michelangelo's work features men like Adam, Moses, Brutus, Apollo, David and Saul. Even when he portrayed the Virgin Mary, it was as a nurturing mother to a full-grown divine male martyr.

Three Grays at the front of the line lock arms. The vibe they send is that of a human barricade against Zola. I know this trio. They are the Troon sisters —Alice, Rabbit, and Cheshire—proud hippie owners of the local head shop called Alice's Wonderland. Their birthdays are five years apart—ages sixty, sixty-five and seventy, respectively. Their skeptical demeanor allows hope to bloom inside me. If they hate this room, Zola's finished. I picture the new, wave-shaped brushed aluminum sign I dreamt about creating for Slaney's business.

The Troon sisters march into Mystick Picnick, jaws tight. Rabbit, the youngest, has a thin streak of gray in her blond curls. She points at the lilac clouds on the foyer ceiling—Zola's homage to Michelangelo's Sistine Chapel.

"This sky is far out," she observes.

Alice, the eldest, cranes her neck upward to view that same ceiling. Her long gray hair grazes the backs of her knees. "Cool chandelier," she states.

Cheshire, the middle sibling in the psychedelic skirt fingers the toile curtain fabric. "Groovy curtains. Good Mystick colors and faces." She turns to me. "Well done, strange woman."

My eyes flare. "No, I . . ."

Zola squeezes me, dolphin gray eyes twinkling. "Snowy's too modest to accept any credit. But I loved working with her on this room. We have so much in common."

I kick her foot and whisper, "No, we don't. Michelangelo was born in the fifteenth century. I love twenty first century design."

"Really?" she asks, stiffly. "Then why have you incorporated Amazon women into your Granite House designs?"

"How do you know what I've designed for Granite House?"

She folds her hands under her chin. "I'm sorry. I should have mentioned that I visited our dear friends, Ivor and Zura, to fast track the fabrication of the basket lighting fixture for this dining room. They mentioned seeing you. They do fine work. Don't you think?"

My body aches from betrayal.

She continues. "I'm bubbling with excitement over putting our names together on a sign. Are we a go?" Several Grays are eavesdropping on our conversation.

"Not yet!" I grind my teeth. "I need to consider whether I'm able to complement your new mission. I will let you know my decision when I'm ready."

As soon as I've spoken, I hear a voice inside my head saying: *What the hell are you thinking? This famous designer will revoke her offer, if you play too hard to get.*

I take a deep breath and introduce Zola to some of the locals whose faces she's included in the toile curtain fabric. People offer me gleeful support. Just as I'm feeling comfortable at a Mystick gathering for the first time, the crowd parts for a humorless Gray in a faded muslin skirt that matches her colorless hair and. I recognize her all too well.

She shakes hands with Zola and acts like I'm invisible. "The name is Nori Moon, Ms. Black. I see you're stealing our local talent." Nori nods in my direction but refuses to make eye contact.

"Guilty as charged." Zola confesses. "I couldn't have created this room design without Snowy."

"No one ever claimed the girl wasn't clever," she says. "That's never been her family's shortcoming. Her grandmother was the best of the Strangeways. I loved her understated designs." Nori storms into Mystick Picnick and performs a quick review. "Not bad." She leans on Zola's shoulder. "This partnership appears to be working. Keep it up."

I start to correct her and Zola pulls me aside. "Lovely, I apologize for lying to Nori Moon about our partnership. I was egotistical enough to think you'd leap at my offer. I wanted us to seem like a team from the get-go." She bites her celestial nail, again. "I'm afraid to say that I also gave that delightful young *Mystick Lights* reporter a premature scoop on our partnership. He just seemed so earnest, though I don't much care for his mother."

"You told Kai that we're partners? You had no right." I clench my fists at my sides.

"Guilty as charged." She bows her head. "How well do you know the young man? Perhaps you, two, should take in a show in The City."

"Brilliant idea," I snort. "I can see it, now. We'll go see 'Harry Potter and the Cursed Child,' and wind up uncomfortable because the subject matter is too close to home."

She laughs, like tinkling bells. "You have such a sense of humor."

"I was raised by strippers. What do you expect?"

Zola tosses back her head and cackles. "See what I mean?"

Visitors shove business cards at Zola and me, begging us to redecorate their homes and offices. These people are all Slaney's clients. Several of them welcome me home. They make me feel like I imagined my status as a town outcast. They assume this partnership is a done deal. One Gray Goddess gushes about how I'm stepping into Slaney's shoes "ever so gracefully"—which I'm definitely not.

Kai pushes through the crowd toward Zola and me, copper pen in hand. "Listen, you two, can I officially announce your partnership?"

Zola grabs Kai and hugs him like she's known him forever. "The ball is in Snowy's court." She woos me with her soothing gray eyes. "The offer I am making is that we split everything fifty-fifty: revenue, lawyer's fees, you name it, for better or for worse, exactly like a good marriage."

"Fifty-fifty?" Kai gags.

"Absolutely," says Zola, warmly.

I barely manage to maintain a poker face, as I've never negotiated a single business deal in my life.

The crowd continues to gossip, while I chew on Zola's offer. I recall Fríða saying that "dramatically timed business announcements generate obscene amounts of revenue." I know that money matters because I remember seeing Mom's face stained with hopelessness when she couldn't save enough cash for us to move out of Mermaid Cottage, into a place of our own.

I slip my white hair smartly behind my ears; adjust my skirt, and grab Zola's microphone. "Fellow Mysticks, may I have your attention? I have the honor of informing you that there is a new design company in town." Zola whips her head around with fake confidence, like we pre-planned this announcement, together. An anxious hush falls over the crowd. "Slaney Strangeways, Decorating, and Zola Black Design have merged to create a new Mystick firm, called . . ."

I pause. It's a trick I learned from the performers at Hips. A dancer's pauses are what make her show sizzle. People love to linger. Anticipation is sexy. Everyone leans in, even Zola. I wait, until I can hear the lapping of the river waves on the shore.

"Our new design firm is called . . . "I pause, again. "Black Snow!" I say, over-articulating. "Our logo will be a black snowflake."

Visitors shriek and hoot at the unexpected name. Of course, I have not consulted Zola on any of this. I thought of this provocative way to combine our names, this very minute. You have to think on your feet in the design world. If Zola is going to manipulate me, I want herto know that I have a few moves of my own.

I step away from the microphone.

"Black Snow?" Kai rubs my arm. "Pretty edgy, Snowy."

"Black Snow!" Zola exclaims, tossing her hands to the heavens, as if she knew it all along.

Zola bats her eyes at me, indicating she's been checked but not checkmated. She retakes command of the microphone and the crowd. "As our new name suggests, Black Snow's designs will focus on humanity and the world as we humans shape it with our art and imaginations. Our work will reflect the soul of humanism."

People clap like thunder.

I mouth the words, "Nice try, Zola" She can't take credit for this crowd's reactions or mood. I worked them up, with that long pause. They would clap at anything.

Kai slips his fingers into mine. "Don't think I didn't see you two dueling for control, just now. You shocked Zola with that ingenious name you dreamed up. Nice move. But how did she twist it around to support her humanist goals?"

I brush my lips across his ear in a whisper, "Zola is more experienced at these sorts of announcements than me. But she won't fool me again."

"You held your own." Kai yanks me into the freshly primed white parlor. All the furniture has been covered in dust cloths. He drags me under the archway by the window that overlooks the river. Its trim is carved with mountain laurel, with most of its pink color chipped off. I'm considering this original color as a launchpad for this room design when Kai presses his mouth into mine. It feels soft, rough, rocky, and wild, new and old at the same time, like the Mystick River. Everything that ever was or will be resides in that kiss.

The door bursts open and we pull apart.

"Here is my young reporter!" coos Zola. "Allow me to offer you an exclusive on my new style focus for your Sunday edition of *Mystick Lights*," she tugs on his driftwood curls. "Unless you're more interested in my sordid tales of tax evasion, recovering substance abuse, and forbidden liaison?"

"Ouch." He taps his head with his copper pen. "You read my editorial."

"I did."

"Allow me to make up for that."

"Certainly."

Kai winks at me, as Zola escorts him away.

I rejoin the crowd, overwhelmed by how many people want me to redo their kitchens. A man's voice shouts my name. I see it's Manny Spellman— sans iron duster, sans pewter boots, sans energy drinks, and even sans energy. His shirtfront is sweat-stained, and his skin carries a bilious green tint.

"Snowy, a private word, please." he pleads.

I picture Moira's lifeless body. "Have you found her?" I ask.

He grabs my arm too hard, like Slaney grabbed it on the day she picked me up from the Mystick Police Station when I was a kid. "

"No," he says. "When I went to the police station today to confront Lara, she was gone," he pants.

"We knew that. I figured she was visiting Clancy. She'll be back."

"No, no." He huffs. "The woman I spoke to said she's gone indefinitely."

"Indefinitely! What?"

"I'll find her. I swear, Lara Oakley will pay for kidnapping Moira and killing your mom!"

Before I can respond, Kai reappears. "Well, if it ain't Sam Spade," he grins. "Lucky for me I needed to grab my notepad for an interview, or I would've missed you." He shoves a photo of Moira and Nahla toward Manny. "So what are you doing to find our missing kids?"

We all stare at the photo. These girls are way too lovely. Their abduction by Clancy and Lara seems like a best-case scenario.

Kai presses the photo into Manny's face. "Well?" he snarls.

"I dunno," he replies.

Kai shoves his business card at Manny. Call me, if you ever have anything useful to share, detective." He enunciates that last word like it's a profanity.

Manny nods. "You do the same," he says, humbly handing Kai his own card.

This is not the glib superhero I met at the Mystick train station. I hate to think Kai was right not to trust Manny. I wonder if I should tell him the truth: that Lara Oakley and Clancy O' Connor have kidnapped Moira O'Connor and Nahla Prakesh, and that Manny and I are after a bad Mystick cop and a cheating, custody-crazed dad. Then I realize I can't tell Kai because I don't have any proof to back up that theory, not just yet.

CHAPTER 12
BLACK SNOW

The warm smoky smell of expensive Italian leather shoes lingers inside Monster House, well after the lawyers have finalized our partnership. Zola's scratchy attitude lingers, as well. She shoos Russ the kitty out of the room, saying she doesn't put up with amateurs. But I don't think her complaint is directed at him. She's mad because I flipped out when she suggested we begin our collaboration by designing her kitchen.

"I can't do it," I plead. "Kitchens have a toxic effect on me. That's why I'm always ordering out for pizza and never cook at home."

"Kitchen designs make money, Lovely," she insists.

"How about we start with the parlor, instead? "I reply. "We can play off of the colorful floral details in the arch overlooking the river, build the room around that water view. I've already got some color options. It's right across from the dining room. What do you say we grow our rooms in pairs, side by side?"

"Grow our rooms?" she sours. "We are not plants. We are human beings. Think Michelangelo, not Rachel Carson. Humans are the heroes of Black Snow's universe. We choose our methods of advancement for practical human benefit. Kitchens showcase domestic technology. That's a human achievement. More important, kitchens are hot, right now. They make MONEY."

She pulls out a spreadsheet with our expenses printed in bright red and lays it on the dining room table. "Look at the costs for the first open house. See how badly we need to profit from a great kitchen? If we standardize a high concept design for national sale, we'll make a fortune. What's your take on kitchen cabinet layouts? You're the expert on shapes."

I remind myself that Zola's not intentionally being insensitive. She may not recall that my mom died while working on this very kitchen. She has no way of knowing that I want to preserve it as her shrine, despite its screaming green color.

I examine Zola's negative spreadsheet again. The numbers boot my kitchen-hating butt into action.

"Fine, we'll design a kitchen," I say, stumbling over that last word.

Zola hugs me. "We are stepping into the future, together, Lovely."

"Stepping into the future," I repeat and snap my fingers. My brain lights up. "That's it. We can reuse the room's old laser green kitchen color for a futuristic feel. I'm thinking Star Trek and Star Wars. Human beings shaping their universe. I'll design some asymmetrical cabinets that challenge nature and enhance them with artificially colored lighting, nothing that hints at sunlight, plants, or natural photosynthesis."

Zola taps her lip. "Asymmetrical cabinets in a kitchen are an edgy choice. Colored lights are very unexpected. I like the way you think outside the box." She flexes her fingers. "However, the green paint is a no-go. Too plantlike. My marketing experts tell me that if I don't move away from plants and animals, the media will claim my "new direction" is nothing but a publicity stunt. That would be bad press. We can't afford that. Rethink the green and we can move forward. Meanwhile, I know you wanted to design the parlor. I promise that will be next. In fact, I'll start thinking about the designs for it, right now."

Russ hops onto the newspaper, and I notice Zola has circled several ads for exotic cats. I pet her kitty and almost let him lick my hand. Looks like, I need to get accustomed to having felines around, as there will likely be *more* cats in this house.

Zola puts of her hands on my white head as if they're a thinking cap. "Lovely, you need to focus. Drum up a theme for our new kitchen that captures the true spirit of Mystick. We need serious buy-in from the locals. Our design must evoke something they adore. Surely you have insights into this subject, as the granddaughter of the great Slaney

Strangeways. What is this town's Holy Grail? What resonates most with Mysticks?"

My eyes gleam. "How about playing to our stereotypes? The Grays are superstitious. People call them witches because they are old women who live independent earthy lives, raise their children lightly, play with herbs and ancient spirituality, and love to cast off their men. I've heard Olde Mystick has more fortunetellers per capita than any other place in America."

"Including Sedona, Arizona?" she asks, stunned.

I scratch my head. "Probably not. East of the Mississippi . . . maybe?" I squint.

"Then let's design an occult kitchen!" Zola's eyes electrify. She wiggles her eager fingers. "Nothing cutesy. Think of superstitions, and spooky things that represent bad omens."

"Mystick Superstition," I confirm. "I love it. How about shattered mirror glass for a mosaic wall around the kitchen dinette?"

"Great!" Zola squeezes her excited fists. "A pale shade of army olive drab will suggest human conquest." She rubs her hands together. "I also have an accent color in mind for a stove that I can't wait to show you."

Zola dashes to another room and returns with a catalogue. She flips to a page marked with a sticky note and slaps her finger on a deep plum stove. "What do you think, Lovely?"

"The purple color reminds me of wampum," she ruminates.

She kisses my head. "You're brilliant. We'll add wampum white and purple to the backsplash in that diamond shape the Indians love. Appealing to the Native American Grays can't hurt." She rubs her thumb and forefingers together. "Now that they have a bit of extra cash from their booming casinos."

My blood burns. I'm surprised to find myself feeling offended by her words, considering I've only just discovered my Native American ancestry.

"What's wrong?" Zola presses. "Don't you like the wampum backsplash idea? Doesn't it complement our theme of superstitions and bad omens?"

"I believe that Wampum is worn for good luck," I correct her.

"Although, the dark purple can signal trouble. And using an actual Native design is appropriation, by the way." I pat the wampum necklace that's secretly tucked under my blouse. "Be careful not to cross that line."

"You possess such keen insights," assesses Zola. "Your indigenous roots are showing."

I've only just discovered I'm Mohegan and already someone is trying to make me into their spiritual consultant. I change the subject. "Maybe we should include black cats in our design. Or is that going too far? You know what people say."

"You mean that some of the Gray Goddesses descend from the survivors of Hartford, Connecticut's seventeenth century witch trials? Its partially true. Alse Critchley descends from Alse Young, the first woman killed for witchcraft in the thirteen colonies."

"Really?" I chuckle. "There's actually something behind this witch-calling nonsense? Go figure."

"Not anything legitimate, if that's what you're asking. Colonial witch-calling was never about devil worship or even true paganism. It was mostly about controlling uppity women who inherited their father's estates or upset their town fathers."

"Then honoring New England's witches is a good thing. So how far do we go with this? Black cats? Or no black cats?" I ask. "I know you don't want to focus on animals."

She pets Russ. "*Familiar* cats are fine. They are associated with humans—*exempli gratia* witches and other light workers. These familiars operate within the boundaries of the human world and under its direction. They're separate from the natural animal world. Some are even famous in human history, like Pyewackett, from England's witch trials, and Manekineko, the Lucky Cat business icon of Japan. Both are bounded by humanity."

Zola draws Pyewackett as a gruff old miser mouser wearing an intriguing amulet and Manekineko as a gangster Buddha kitty.

"These are amazing!" I say, realizing how she got to be so famous. "They will look great on wallpaper." I run my hands through my secretly graying hair. "Let's add some fortunetelling elements."

I sketch a graduated crystal ball light trio for the kitchen.

Zola leans over for a peek and lights up. "This is tremendous,

Snowy. I knew you would be the ideal partner."

Feeling sparked, I keep going, drawing dishes decorated with stone runes and tea cups with tarot designs.

"How very marketable!" Zola squeals.

I go one step further and draw a cauldron. "This is for the fireplace."

She pulls that paper to her cheek. "I love the cauldron. We can create a line of black kitchenware called Mystick Cauldron. Witches Smitches. People love them. What would Halloween be without the old gals? Create a fun shape for the handle of our large fireplace cauldron. Shapes are your strong suit." Zola drifts toward the stairs.

"I'll contact the Mystick Seaport blacksmith to discuss ideas," I suggest. "He can forge it. We can fill it with bright green granny smith apples on the day of Mistick Superstition's showcase."

Zola is already writing purchase orders and misses, just as I had hoped. Those apples are my discreet tribute to Rebekah Strangeways' bright green kitchen. Speaking of apples, I need to order plenty of local hard cider for our event. The Grays love it, andit may soften the critics. After all, making fun of the leading women in town is a risky business.

CHAPTER 13
MYSTICK SUPERSTITION

An endless line of Grays streams through our Mystick Superstition room showcase. Zola signs contract after contract, success trailing off her pen like fairy dust. From the loud speakers, Stevie Wonder's bewitching voice wails—

> *When you believe in things that you don't understand,*
> *Then you suffer, Superstition ain't the way . . .*

The song fades out. The air thickens and deadens, like I've entered the shades of gray. A woman stumbles in, carrying a swaddled baby. No, not a baby, a cat. A frayed yellow ribbon hangs over the sleeve of her blouse which is covered with food stains that look like they've been there for days. It takes me a moment to realize this disheveled woman is my Aunt Selkie, Moira's mom.

I hug her, inhaling the putrid stench of abject misery.

"You didn't have to come, Selkie," I say.

Aisling tries to wriggle out of her blanket.

The crowd thins like a radioactive dust cloud has descended. Zola rushes around, trying to finalize deals. I remain glued to my aunt's side, hoping she will speak.

"I'm glad you didn't cancel your open house," she says, finally, "just because of the new development in Moira's case."

"What new development?" I ask, holding my breath.

"You didn't hear? They found Moira's foghorn."

Aisling escapes from her blanket, leaps into my arms, and claws me.

"No one could separate Moira from her foghorn," I say, pulling cat claws out of my arm. "Where did Manny find it?"

"Manny who?" Flames flash in Selkie's eyes. "That creep hasn't visited or called since the day he took off with you. He's a fly-by-nighter, like the sleazeballs your mom used to slum around with."

"Who found it, then?" I gulp.

"One of the local beat cops discovered it by a drainage ditch. Chief Oakley called to tell me about it this morning."

A hot flush of shame comes over me. "Chief Oakley is back? Manny said she left town."

"Manny, Manny, Manny," she mocks. "Manny's an idiot. Lara took off for a few days for her chemotherapy treatments. People love to count her out. But she wouldn't let cancer slow her down, for long. She's a lot like Slaney in that way."

My gut feels hollow. Manny misled me by pointing the finger at Lara, when she's not healthy enough to have participated in a kidnaping plot. His smoking gun photo of Clancy kissing her may have been nothing more than him wishing her well before her cancer treatments. I've wasted precious time following Manny Spellman's red herrings.

I pull Zola away from a customer and whisper. "I need to get in touch with Manny."

"You have the same contact information for him that I do," she disdains, then whips her head around. "Wait. Is there some new development regarding Moira?" She grips my hand, hard.

"Ouch. Yes," I reply.

"Whatever it is, this is not the time to discuss it. There's nothing that can be done in the middle of our showcase." She straightens her linen sheath, painted with the tarot card that represents the moon. "This is a business affair," she ices. "Soldier on."

"Screw you," I say, storming upstairs to her bedroom to use the phone.

The walls are newly painted in white primer.Except for the gorgeous redwood Parnian desk in the corner, this room looks like an asylum.

Manny's phone goes straight to voice mail. I tough out the last hour of the showcase and leave without speaking to Zola. Tossing under my bedsheets, I can't stop thinking about the fact that the now-vanished

Manny Spellman pointed me toward misleading evidence. He's the one who claimed Clancy O'Connor had an affair with Police Chief Lara Oakley, which in turn made me forget that Moira might be in real danger, captured by someone other than her dad. Now I can't reach Manny, and Lara has returned. I think about how Manny offered to help me find Moira and then shifted his focus to Mom's murder case. Why would he want to distract me from finding Moira? Is Kai right in saying Manny is gunning for Lara's job, hoping to make her look bad? Could Manny be trying to discredit the Mystick Police by ensuring they fail to find a kidnapped child? That's beyond sick. Yet Manny disappeared the moment he could no longer pretend Lara ran off with Clancy. I was set up. I chug the bottle of leftover hard cider I grabbed on my way out of Monster House.

A supernova of sunshine and a ringing telephone erupt inside my pounding head. I grapple for the receiver and knock over the empty cider jug.

"Good morning!" Selkie perks. "You won't believe it! Fifty thousand dollars in cash just arrived. Fifty thousand dollars wrapped in shamrock tissue paper, with a note that says, 'This is a gift to ease the blow of what I took from you, and I don't just mean the girl.' Isn't this great news! Clancy has Moira. She's safe, Snowy! Moira is safe!"

"Moira is safe?" My words drift into the receiver. "What? How?"

"It seems Clancy found a new woman and ran off with her and our kid. Not much of a surprise there. I guess I should have expected this. For the first time, I'm actually glad to hear it."

My heart skips a beat. "What about Nahla?"

"I forgot to tell you, yesterday. The police got a tip saying Nahla's dad took her away so she wouldn't be around when her addict mom is released from rehab. Both girls are okay! They're really okay!"

"That's great, Selkie, I say, trying to process this news. You should go to mass and say a prayer. Have a great day."

I grab the morning paper. For the first time in weeks I'm not terrified by what I might read. Turns out, I should be. Kai Corby's review of yesterday's open house is not what you'd expect from a guy who just kissed you.

Superstition Ain't the Way

Black Snow's latest room showcase features ridiculous cats and a ghoulish purple and army drab color scheme. The saving grace is that this collaboration between Zola Black and Snowy Strangeways remains new. I say we forgive these great gals this one indiscretion, as long as they redeem themselves with their next design.

I'm the poison in the bad brew known as Superstition. I screwed up this room because of my personal issues with kitchens. I phone Zola to apologize.

"Have you read the paper?" I ask.

"Yes, Lovely," she sighs. "I accept full responsibility for this failure. That adorable young reporter is right. Whatever was I thinking? Mystick Superstition's colors evoke images of war, putrefaction, and bad luck. You'll notice he didn't attack your cabinets, or your layout, or your furnishings. He targeted my bad color choices, and he was right to do so. I deserve every foul thing he can hurl at me."

I'm speechless because I realize that what she's saying is accurate: Kai's criticism focused on Zola's mistakes, not mine. But as I'm a partner in this design firm; I should have trusted my instincts and pushed to keep Mom's green. I'm not a kid anymore. I have to remember that everything that goes into and comes out of Black Snow is attached to my name and pocketbook.

Still, this bad review is much worse for Zola than me. She never gets bad reviews. It might be enough to make her quit our partnership. She has nothing to keep her here but a shaky new business that's downgrading her brand. I have multiple reasons to stay, beyond my commitment to Black Snow. I have a murder and a kidnapping to solve. A father and grandfather that need tracking down. I also need to find out why Manny misled me. I should never have accepted his claim that the words on Mom's chest represent obscure song lyrics. I knew they meant something more. The fact that I saw a guy shouting "Do as you must" means something, regardless of what Manny says. The overturned clogs at Mom's murder scene mean something, as well. At the very least, they represent a Native American custom. I need to investigate the shouting man and that Native superstition about overturned shoes. The newspaper says the Mohegan Wigwam Festival is happening this weekend. I know where I plan to go, next.

CHAPTER 14
WELCOME TO THE CIRCLE

The sweet scent of red cedar hits me as soon as I enter the Mohegan Reservation. These peaceful grounds on the Thames River contrast with the military-industrial landmarks that cover most its banks—like the United States Coast Guard Academy, the Naval Submarine Base, Electric Boat Submarine Plant, and several post-apocalyptic scrap metal heaps.

After we park in the visitor parking area, Zola starts blinking. I wonder if she's blinking back tears of joy, over the natural beauty of this place. Then I realize she's taking in the glittering silver sequins of the fancy dancers, and the celery and carrot-colored fringe of the grass dancers, the neon vests of the parking attendants. These are unsentimental blinks, like the shutter of a camera going off, taking in light, shade, and cast. I head for the vendor area and buy a tee shirt that says "Wolf People," while Zola stops at a booth selling Pendleton blankets. Moments later, she's fumbling for something inside her handbag, with a blanket stuffed under one arm.

"Damn it!" she yells. "I left my phone in my other bag. Lovely, you stay here and enjoy all this."

"You're not coming back. Are you?" I ask.

She licks her lips. "I'm sure young Mr. Corby will be happy to offer you a lift home."

I pretend to look disgusted. But I'm actually grateful for the chance to privately investigate my Mohegan roots. I cruise the dance circle under the big white tent. Clusters of men pound huge drums, surrounded by clouds of sage, sweetgrass, and cedar smoke. According to Gertie, cedar is the most powerful of the three. I can't help thinking that is why Mom gave me that name which I discarded because I did not know about my Native ancestry

A kid with hair shaved everywhere but on top posts a sign that lists the order for The Grand Entry dancers. I'm reading it, when someone says, "Will you look who's come home to Mohegan!"

I turn and call, "Gertie!"

There's more gray in her hair than the last time I saw her. But she is resplendent in her buckskin dress and seeing her makes this place feel like home.

She wraps her a pink shawl around me. "Mohegan welcomes you," she calls out to the surrounding landscape. Her words remind me of the first time Lyr greeted me at Granite House. These Grays like to personify places, to give them life and agency of their own. I think about Mystick. It definitely carries its own spirit.

"I hear I am Mohegan's long-lost daughter." I say.

"Absolutely. Your grandfather was my brother, Wolfie."

I hug her. "I can't believe you never told me."

"I never spoke of it while your grandmother was alive, out of respect for her wishes. Now that she has passed away, I would like us to dance together in the circle."

Before I can explain that I don't know any tribal dance steps, the Master of Ceremonies moves in, shaking a fist at me. He's wearing a wampum beaded vest with jeans and fully beaded moccasins.

"She can't dance in our circle," he derides.

Gertie turns her back on him and tightens the shawl around me. "Snowy, I need to speak to your know-nothing uncle." She points to a familiar girl with spiked boy-band hair with a shock of gray, cargo shorts, a vest with a gazillion pockets, and a cast on her leg. "Would you mind visiting with your cousin, Lightning, for a few moments?"

"Lightning!" I call out, rushing towards the waitress I met at the Silver Moon.

She's whittling a stick with an antler-handle knife and points the knife tip at me. "Told ya I'd see you back on the rez." She sticks the knife into her cast. "Too bad I'm too laid up to make much mischief."

"You knew we were related, all along. Didn't you?" I sit in the empty plastic lawn chair beside her.

"Did I know that the Supreme Gray Goddess's granddaughter, the chick with the glam makeup, sno-cone hair, designer duds, and false eyelashes was my relative? Hell yeah, Gertie told me. She also told me you're working on Lyr Corby's Granite House interiors. As an architect, I'm more interested in the house's exterior."

"What would you change?"

"That house needs a nice glass rear atrium, facing the river. It would lighten and brighten the place up."

"You think Lyr Corby would go for it?"

"No, but she can't live forever." Lightning's face turns suspicious. "Wait a minute. Lyr only hires Grays." She points to my hair. "I told you that you'd turn soon. When did it happen?"

"Not long after I saw you at Slaney's funeral. My transition felt like a bad allergic reaction. Big pink spots broke out on my arms and legs."

Lightning cackles, "The same thing happened to me. I think I'm somehow responsible for all of these early transitions. They started happening as soon as I began messing with the old stuff."

"The old stuff?"

"Some of our ancient ceremonies. You have to be careful with the old stuff. That's how I messed up my leg."

"What did you do?"

"Since you don't even know Indian 101, glam girl, I'll wait a bit before I hit you with any advanced lessons."

"Fair enough."

Lighting points to a pair of moccasins with raspberry beaded trim that lay upside down on a blanket by her chair. "What do you think of these?" she asks.

"The color is hot," I say, not mentioning that her beadwork technique could stand to improve. "Why do you turn them over?"

"For protection. Why do you ask?"

"Somebody turned my mom's clogs upside down, after she was murdered. I've seen Gertie do something similar to my shoes. Why would a killer do that?"

Lightning sits up, more serious. "Whoever turned over your Mom's clogs was trying to bless her journey to the Spirit World. That person didn't kill her."

I bite my lip, relieved that Mom experienced some blessing upon her death, considering she received no Irish keening or Mohegan burial rites.

"So Mom's clogs weren't flipped over by her killer," I conclude. "Thanks, Lightning. I owe you one."

"Great!" She lifts up the moccasins. "I'm calling in that favor, right now. I need someone to dance for me, to help heal my leg."

I slip them on. "I'm glad the girls from Hips aren't here," I grunt.

"Hips?" Lightning raises her hands.

I rub my nose. "The strip club where I was raised. My nannies used to say soft flat shoes were only for women under the age of ten.

"Fascinating. I have actually seen beaded Native fashion stilettos but not stiletto moccasins," Lightning remarks. "The whole point of them is to connect your feet to the earth."

"I get that: the power of connection and ceremony," I agree, recalling how the years fell off Alse Critchley when she drew energy from Slaney's funeral crowd.

Gertie returns, beaming at the sight of me wearing Lightning's moccasins. She points to a nearby drum group, whose members are chewing some kind of root to prepare their throats for singing. "Grand Entry is about to begin," she advises.

"I'm going to dance for Lightning's bad leg," I explain.

"Let's practice the toe-heel step." She demonstrates the footwork, en route to the Grand Entry circle.

Lightning shakes a gourd rattle from the sidelines. I slow my pace so as not to get ahead of Gertie. We dance like this is something we do all the time, like it's no big deal. But it's a humungous, ginormous, super-colossal deal. My grandma kept my Mohegan heritage from me all my life. Now presto, I'm one of the tribe,wearing a borrowed pink shawl with toe-scrunching moccasins with heels so flat my calves want to scream. But my spirit is bursting, as I dance with hundreds of my people in a spiral under a big white tent. I'm following a line that coils, tighter and tighter, as hundreds more dancers join the line. I love the walloping drumbeat, the stampede of feet, the hooting cries, the flying fringe, the closeness of the crowd.

I've never felt so much a part of anything. The girls at Hips were great dancers but Fríða never let me dance with them. Here, I'm at the center of a dance circle that connects me to my family, our planet, and the universe. I'm sweaty and uncomfortable. I have no idea when this will end. But Lightning's radiant face tells me that this dance may be helping her.

I swear I hear the wind whisper, "Welcome to the circle."

The song concludes with a heavy thump of the drum. I'm dazed as I thank Gertie and hand the mocs back to Lightning.

"Hold up." Lightning scribbles her email and cell number on the sole with a sharpie and returns the moccasins to me. "You've earned these. I gave you my contact info so we can stay in touch. Now all you need to do is wear those mocs out of here and their medicine will fully take effect for me."

My jaw is dangling. "Are you bullshitting me? Do I really have to wear these for your leg to heal?"

"Absolutely."

"Why?"

"Because seeing Snowy Strangeways wear flat mocs out into the world will give me a good laugh, and laughter is great medicine."

"Indians!" I grumble playfully.

"Right back at you, cousin."

The Master of Ceremonies steps in front of me and I get a better look at his wampum beaded vest. There are three diamond shapes on the back and I can't take my eyes away from them.

"Not bad dancing for a first-timer," he mumbles.

"Is that all you have to say to the grandniece you haven't seen in years?" asks Gertie. "Do something good for a change, Lake Mazeen. Be a proper great uncle. Tell the girl about her family."

"Did you know my dad?" I ask.

His eyes continue to steer clear of mine. Yet I can't help but notice they're the same crow black color.

He snorts. "Rebekah was troubled. It's hard to say who your dad was. Her behavior drove your grandfather crazy. She used Wolfie's tribal teachings for dark purposes. Slaney thought Wolfie was crazy to claim their daughter dabbled in bad medicine. She sided with Rebekah on everything. That girl hated this reservation because we conducted healing ceremonies to help cleanse her. Slaney said we were too harsh on Rebekah. If we'd been harsher, Rebekah might still be alive. So might ..." He wrings his hands. "Your grandmother, Slaney, claimed we abused Rebekah, by making her sweat, fast, and purge. We were only trying to save her life. Slaney was blind to the girl's faults, until it was too late. Now you know your whole ugly family story." Lake turns and walks away.

"Wait! I get that Slaney didn't want me to meet you because of the ceremonies you performed on Mom. But you must know something about my mysterious dad."

He snorts like a bull. "Your mom got pregnant at sixteen and wouldn't disclose the father of her baby. Blind ambition was her only true love. That's how she managed to piss off the only adult whobelieved in her—your grandmother, Slaney. Wolfie moved away to keep her darkness from latching onto him.

"Let me get this straight. My mom was connected to this reservation and then left it because she went bad, like some fallen angel?"

"More like an evil spirit," says Lake.

He turns away, and I grab the fringe of his vest. Lake eyes me frostily. I let go, recalling that it's disrespectful to touch a Native person's regalia.

"I'm sorry," I say. "But you don't seem happy to see me, Great Uncle Lake. You won't even look at me. How come?"

He clenches his jaw. "The truth? You're a carbon copy of Rebekah—except for the phony bleached hair and mile-high legs. She was a trial to my brother and our tribe. That's what makes it difficult for me to look at you. Fortunately, I hear that physical appearance is where your similarity to Rebekah ends. My Pequot cousin, Lyr Corby, says good things about you. Her adopted son is a good man. Though I hear you've discovered that on your own," he winks. "Too bad nothing can come of your relationship with him."

Those last words hit me like a slap. I remember Lyr saying much the same thing. ""What do you mean nothing can come of our relationship?" I ask.

Gertie swats his arm.

"That's Gray business. It's not my place to say." He marches off. Gertie follows him, cursing.

A crying kid with red face paint wipes his tears and shmears the paint onto his hand. Then he uses that hand to tug on my shawl. I cringe.

"Have you seen River?" he asks. "Do you know where he went?" The boy's eyes are desperate, "I've got to find him!"

"I don't know anyone named River. I'm sorry." I try to leave but he hugs me and more red paint stains my shirt. "Please, we have to find him."

I shake him off. "Fine, kid. I'll take you to the podium so the MC can make an announcement," I warily grab his clammy hand and bring him to Lake.

"This boy says his friend, River, is missing," I explain.

Lake yells to the arena director to go get Gertie. He announces on the mic, "We have a missing child, named River Mazeen. He's a skinny kid with blue eyes, and a long brown braid. Please tell a staff member if you see him."

Gertie is already yelling at the tribal police to hurry up and find the boy.

Lake turns to me, his face fierce. "Snowy, River is Gertie's grandchild, my great nephew, your cousin." He punches the air. "You come to Mohegan and look what happens. You're bad medicine. Just like your mother."

"Stop it!" I scream. "I know you're upset over River going missing. But I didn't like Rebekah any more than you did."

He stomps the ground. "How do I know you're not cut from the same cloth? It's important to stop people like her before they become too dangerous. I failed once and can't let that happen again." His voice grows hoarse. "When someone crosses the line, you do as you must." He storms over to the tribal police to talk to Gertie.

"Do as you must?" I echo, dumbstruck.

I dry heave onto the ground. Manny was wrong about those fateful words being simple song lyrics. Lake Mazeen just spoke them in a powerfully vindictive way. It's no coincidence that they were written in blood on Mom's chest. Lake hated Mom. Hated her enough to want her dead, enough to want me dead. I've just moved Lake Mazeen's name to the top of the list of devils who may have murdered Rebekah Strangeways.

PART III
WHO KILLED REBEKAH STRANGEWAYS?

CHAPTER 15
RIVER OF TRUTH

Kai's old-school Land Rover pulls up to the red cedars that line the entrance to the Mohegan Reservation. His vehicle is equipped with a winch, axe, ladder and raised wheels with alligator treads. Considering the fact that he lives on a rocky dirt path in old growth woods filled with bears, these accessories make sense.

He eyes me with horror. I examine myself to see what's wrong. Oh, hell on hot rollers! My ankles and feet are filthy from dancing in dirt. My shawl and shirt are covered with red face paint stains. I fold my arms over them.

"Sorry about the last-minute shout-out for a ride." I say, frazzled. "But another kid's gone missing."

"I heard about the missing Mohegan boy on the scanner. I'm very sorry."

"That's not all the news. Turns out my mystery grandfather was a Mohegan. I got to meet his brother, my great uncle, Lake Mazeen, and I think he murdered my mom."

"What? Hop in." he says. "We need to get to the Mystick Police station."

Kai crushes the speed limit, as I rasp out my report of what's happened. "Turns out I'm the grandniece of this Mohegan guy named Lake Mazeen, and he hated my mom. He couldn't stand looking at me, due to my resemblance."

"Nice."

"He also spoke the same words that were written on Mom's dead body."

"That's creepy as hell. Maybe he took the boy from the reservation."

"I doubt it. The kid's his nephew."

"I can't believe there are three missing kids, now." He lowers his head. "Three!"

I flush. "Oh no! I forgot to tell you. Moira is safe with her dad. So is Nahla. Clancy paid Selkie fifty thousand dollars, as compensation for taking their daughter. She seems okay with that. There's only one missing kid and it's River."

"I doubt that," he says, jerking the Land Rover onto the side of the road.

"What are you stopping?" I yelp.

"I need to concentrate. I can't imagine where Clancy would get that kind of money."

"From his rich new girlfriend, I presume."

"No way. Even if this 'rich new girlfriend' story is true, Clancy O'Connor would never give away that much cash. He was a petty thief before he married Selkie."

"But he loves Moira."

"Maybe not more than money."

"Who else would send money to Selkie?"

"Moira's real kidnappers, of course. They may be trying to cut a sneaky deal for her silence, figuring she's loopy on drugs and booze and will fall for anything. It looks like they succeeded. Who knows what they've done to that poor kid. As far as I'm concerned, three kids remain missing."

I shake my head, no. "No way. Not all three. Selkie said the police got a tip saying Nahla's dad took her out of town because he didn't want her around when her addict mom is released from rehab. Nahla is fine."

"Maybe."

"Either way, we better hurry." I yank on my hair, picturing Moira locked in some stranger's basement.

We squeal back onto the road. I don't breathe until we see Lara, signing paperwork at the station. Mary Bird takes one look at my hot mess of an outfit and starts laughing.

Lara jabs a finger at Kai. "I see the press is here. Is this discussion on the record?"

He gives her the all-clear sign. "I'm not here as a reporter. I'm here as Snowy's friend. Nothing we discuss will see print. You know I'm loyal to the Grays."

"That, you are," confirms Lara.

Lara directs us to her office and tries to close the imperfect blinds. She appears paler and smaller than the last time I saw her.

"First, I need to apologize," I say to her. "I was foolish to follow Manny Spellman's advice. He gave me false leads in Moira's case. He told me you were his prime suspect, due to your romantic relationship with Clancy."

She wags a weak finger from behind her desk. "Former relationship, and I'd hardly call it romantic. Besides, Manny is a funny one to talk about secret relationships."

"You know Manny?"

She flutters her eyes. "Manny has quite the romantic history in Mystick. I'd call it a legacy, in fact. Big, bad, charming Manny Spellman comes and goes from this town like a nor'easter. He should understand the fickle nature of Clancy O'Connor. I don't think any woman has ever enjoyed a 'romantic relationship' with either Manny or Clancy. Don't get me wrong. I love Clancy. He can show a woman a fine time. Manny only brings trouble. Given a choice between the two, I'll take Clancy, any day."

Kai elbows me. "What'd I tell you, Snowy? You can't trust that Manny guy."

I push him away. "Lara, I'm here for two reasons. First, because there's been an important development in Moira's case. Second, because I met someone on the Mohegan Reservation who may have killed my mom. Third, because there's another missing kid."

Lara withdraws a half-full bottle of Jameson whiskey and three cloudy glass tumblers from a drawer. "We all need a drink." She pours us each a glass.

Nobody ever remembers that I'm only eighteen.

"Here's to the three of us working together to solve these crimes," Lara sips the glass with blue lips and her face relaxes.

I push the glass away. "I need to confess something. I haven't kept you informed about developments regarding Moira because I thought you were responsible for her disappearance."

Lara's expression prunes.

The whiskey in front of me appears suddenly irresistible. I guzzle it and bang the glass on Lara's desk. "Selkie received fifty thousand dollars. She thinks it came from Clancy as payment for taking Moira."

"I already know about that money." she says.

Kai and I exchange shocked glances. "Okay, fine," I say. "But we don't think it came from Clancy."

Lara pats my hand. "Neither do I. I also don't believe Clancy abducted Moira. We, Grays, have eyes and ears everywhere. The missing kid cases are our primary concern. I've got half a dozen officers on them." She turns to the corner of the room, like there's some hidden camera or person, that we need to avoid. "As far as your mom's murder goes, we should discuss that elsewhere. Let's take a walk cross the street to the river."

Kai and I watch Lara drag her weak legs across River Road like a half-squished bug. She fumbles to remove her clogs and sits on a rock. Her blue-veined feet dangle in the rippling water. I slip off my moccasins and lay them on the cool grass, upside down. Kai and I awkwardly share a second rock and dip our feet in. I'm grateful to wash off the powwow dust.

Lara hops into the water and points at my head. "Now that you're a Gray, your actions are part of our circle. We can speak plainly, here, in the River of Truth."

"River of Truth?" snorts Kai. "Snowy's not a Gray. She doesn't know about all of your ridiculous superstitions."

He touches my hair. "Right, Snowy?"

"Actually Kai, Snowy has recently taken her place among us." Lara points to the river. "And as a Gray cannot lie, once she steps into the river."

"She's only eighteen. How is that possible?" He slumps like he's been punched.

"Young Grays seem to be a trend for the new millennium," confides Lara.

I keep my feet in the river but refuse to jump in. "Moving on," I say, kicking the water. "I suspect my grandfather's brother, Lake Mazeen, of killing my mom. He hated her. Plus, I heard him speak the same phrase I saw written on her chest at her murder scene." I heave a sigh. "Although, I know you think there was nothing written on her chest."

"I saw the writing on Rebekah's chest," says Lara. "I denied it, until now, because you were not part of our Gray circle."

I bite my lip till it bleeds. "You now admit that Mom's killing was ritual, just like I always claimed." Something boils inside me.

"Yes, it was a ritual killing. But Lake Mazeen didn't do it. It was a Gray killing."

"What? A Gray killing? You better tell me who did it. If you don't, I'll reveal your past relationship with Clancy to your superiors. You'll lose your job. You'll lose your medical insurance. I know you're ill and . . ."

"Whoa! Down girl," cautions Kai.

A cawing sound overhead breaks the tension and draws our eyes, up to three flying crows.

Lara waves her frail hand at me like a handkerchief in the wind. "Here is Macha, right on time!"

"The goddess of war." I recall.

"And the goddess of peace," corrects Lara. "The two are inseparable. Macha also has two sisters, Madb and Morrigan, who increase her conjuring power. Three is a powerful number."

"Fine, maybe the three of us can come up with some answers," I assent, hopping into the river, soaking my jeans. The rocky river bottom is slippery, jagged, unsteady, a lot like my world.

"How much do you know about our Gray connection to the river, Snowy?"

I recite the Gray chant that Slaney taught me as a child: "*Rivers know all things—past, present, and future. Flowing like time, they are endlessly cleansing, with occasional ripples of dark tides. We, Grays, stand as a force of light against those dark tides, maintaining the balance, the shades of gray.*"

"Impressive," mumbles Kai.

Lara splashes water at me.

"Hey!" My arms and face tingle from the cold.

"This cool salty water will stir your memory and bring out the truth," she says. Do you recall the naked bathing woman who collapsed near you at Slaney's funeral?"

"Of course. What about her?"

"She collapsed because she lied to her friends, while wading naked in the river. It was lucky the paramedics were able to resuscitate her."

"People don't stop breathing for lying in the river," snickers Kai. "That's some serious Gray horseshit. The river doesn't have a mind of its own."

"All of Mother Earth has a mind of its own!" Lara retorts. "The land, the stones, the trees . . ."

"You sound like a Native American Gray," I murmur.

"I'm not. But Supreme Gray Fox Edith Wyouggs is my aunt by marriage," Lara replies. "Edith has taught me that the earth is alive, and we must connect to its life force." She turns to Kai. "But, as the earth is also a woman, it's harder for men to make that connection."

"Sexist much?" Kai folds his arms. "Sometimes, you Grays can be serious man-haters."

"I'll admit that some of our Gray practices need reconsideration," admits Lara, "like the fact that Rebekah Strangeways was ritually murdered."

I pull myself unsteadily back up onto the rock. One of the three crows lands beside Kai. The other two crows land on either side of me.

Kai draws air through his teeth.

"I stare at my reflection in the river. "I'm guessing Rebekah was killed by the Grays for something worse than lying in the river. She must have broken a major Gray law. That's the only way Lyr would authorize her execution."

"You are mostly correct," says Lara, caressing the water. "If a Gray falls victim to the worst aspect of The Gray Curse, the Rede requires that we punish her. It instructs us to 'Do as you must.'"

"Do as you must. Those were the words written on Mom's chest."

"Precisely."

Kai shivers. "I should leave. This is privileged Gray information."

"No Kai, please stay," insists Lara. "You've lived in the shadow of the Grays all of your life. Men don't fare well around us. We treat them far too poorly. I'd like to see that change, so I'm including you in this discussion as a first step."

"Thank you," he replies, frightening the crows off the rock.

"Listen Lara," I say. "If Mom broke the Rede and Lyr heard the case, someone else must have brought the charges. Mom was Native. So she also violated the Qutuhikan. But I'm guessing Gertie didn't bring charges against her. They were too close."

The screech of an eagle keeps Lara from responding. We all look up and see the bird getting mobbed by the crows who just left our side.

"Eagles are a sign of purity and high ideals," I note. "And they're angry. So you must be leaving something out, Lara. You need to speak the whole truth."

She keeps staring at the sky. "You're right. Gertie did not charge Rebekah with a violation of the *Qutuhikan*, the line that cannot be crossed. It was Supreme Gray Fox Edith Wyouggs who did that."

"Edith? Was Mom somehow involved in Lucy Wauby's disappearance?"

"Yes."

"Even if Mom kidnapped the child, I don't believe she should have been executed," I say.

"Or you don't believe in the death penalty when it involves your mom?" asks Lara.

"I don't believe in it, period."

The eagle screams, louder than before. A flurry of eagle feathers falls on us like rain. Crows don't attack eagles. I catch a falling tail feather and hold it tight, feeling stronger.

"It's complicated," Lara explains.

The crows begin cawing. I look up and don't see the eagle, anymore. But another white eagle feather drifts down, this one onto Lara's shoulder. She hands it off to me. Kai notices that a third eagle feather has fallen beside him. He hands it to me. I now grip the three eagle feathers and feel stronger than I've felt in my entire life.

"Rebekah's executioner is the one who wrote on her chest," says Lara.

I almost drop the feathers, sensing I'm about to discover the truth about who killed Mom.

Lara continues. "Riley Finch served as the executioner's assistant, which is why he and Slaney had a falling out."

"Riley helped kill Mom?" I shake all three feathers at Lara, my hand gripping them so tight my palm sweats. "There's only one way you can know all this, Lara Oakley. You're the Gray executioner. You're the one who slit my mom's throat!"

CHAPTER 16
GRANDMOTHER MOON

I skip my normal mourning rituals of shower and makeup, drag on a pair of old jeans, my Mohegan wigwam wolf tee shirt, and worn ballet flats. My crazy life is beginning to make sense for the first time, and the truth is pitch black, like the heart of this town. Slaney had good reason to freak when I got hauled into the Mystick Police Station at age ten. The Gray Executioner who killed Mom was the same cop who arrested me. My grandma feared I'd wind up like her daughter. The differences between us were few. I looked like Mom. I enjoyed painting and interior design, like Mom. I took risks for my art and got in trouble with the law, like Mom. Mine are the same habits that led Mom to fall prey to The Gray Curse, violate the Rede and Quitihikan, and get executed.

It's no use trying to focus on work. I can't work for Lyr. She's the one who sentenced Mom. What was I thinking, covering her hideous weapon's case with chainmail? Chainmail is archaic, like her laws. Where did I get the idea to design a room featuring ancient Amazon women and a chandelier shaped like one of their outdated bows? I'm a twenty-first century designer. Were these designs inspired by my old-fashioned Gray values?

Everything I put together for Granite House is now junk. My whole life is junk, like right after Mom died. Only this time, a change of name and hair color won't fix it. I hate Mystick's fake adorability. This whitewashed colonial town is full of violent old women who operate outside of mainstream law. Sure, kidnapping is bad. But how can I be sure Mom was guilty? Maybe the Grays framed her due to her free-spirited nature. Either way, they executed her without the benefit of a lawyer to represent her side of the case.

The Grays need to consider their roots. English colonial soldiers burned down the Pequot village on this river over rumors that the Native inhabitants killed one of their traders. They ignored the Pequot side of the story and their aboriginal right to this land. The Grays claim they were founded to end that sort of injustice. But if they killed mom without giving her a fair trial, are they really any better?

Gray families are not even real families. Our family photos are always missing fathers, and there may as well be no mothers. Gray women lack the ability to nurture anyone. They're so busy controlling their enclaves and obsessing about their art that they forget about the safety and happiness of their offspring. The fact that I had loving nannies to care for me made me better off than most Gray kids. Hell, I was better off than most kids, period.

I stand in front of Slaney's self-portrait that shows her trapped inside a glass box and begin to wonder if it contains some hidden meaning. I know this painting mattered to Slaney because she insisted that it remain in Mermaid Cottage, even if I sold the place. I consider the lit beeswax candle sticking out of her pocket. It reminds me of the beeswax candles in her design barn.

I head into the barn and find a pile of punched tin covers, lying on the floor. I place them over the lit beeswax candle sconces. Light beams shoot out the holes in the tin, creating lines of light that intersect at a point on the one bare wall in this room, not cluttered with seaside knickknacks.

I feel around that bare wall and something clicks. A panel the size of a small door pops open. I expect to discover a hidden closet, filled with dusty books about ancient Celtic goddesses or a pile of secret love letters and photos that might tell me more about my grandfather. But all I find behind this door is blackness. When my eyes adjust, I notice it opens onto a spiral staircase. I descend those stairs, forcing myself not to fall into a vision and tumble.

Halfway down, I catch a familiar smell. It's sage smoke, telling me this space has recently been used for some sort of Gray ceremony. I kick the wall. Dammit. My barn is a Gray gathering space!

At the bottom of the stairs, I light a large whale oil lantern that's hanging from the ceiling. Its caramel glow reveals a room with ash gray walls, an oyster gray ceiling, and a graphite gray floor. Everything in here is black, white, or some shade of gray, like an old television show, or a scene from a nightmare. At least I now know who buys all the old-school candles and lanterns from those shops, downtown. I light a trio of thick white candles that are set on a tall wrought iron stand. Their light reveals a wall covered with square steel-framed pictures of men in gray coats. One photo catches my eye. It shows a guy with sharp features and a ponytail. Something about him looks familiar. Then it hits me. This is Manny Spellman! He's younger, unbald, and less of a workout fiend, but I'd recognize him, anywhere.

The plaque above his photo and those of the other men in gray coats says "Heralds."

What's a herald?

I light the three white candles in the pewter holder on a second wall. They illuminate hundreds of tiny oval pewter frames. The plaque above this grouping reads "Gray Goddesses." I scan the faces but don't see Mom. One frame is turned over. I don't dare look at it. I notice my face is not among these images and wonder if I'm soon expected to participate in some sort of special sisterhood photo shoot.

I light another group of candles in a white gold stand beside a third wall. Here I find a circle of white gold frames. They are diamond-shaped and assembled under a plaque that says "Supreme Gray Goddesses." I recognize Alse's photo, right away, even though she appears to have been very young when she first became a Gray leader, perhaps in her twenties.

A giant Lucite candelabra full of candles sits on a table in front of the fourth wall. Once lit, the candles reveal a line of photos framed in black lacquer crescent moon shapes. A carved plaque on top says "Ombudswomen." These women stand out with their New York hair and makeup, in contrast to the sun-bronzed, ocean-kissed, long-haired Grays Goddesses.

An easel in a nearby corner contains a single tarnished silver frame, with a photo of a yacht filled with friendly waving women that's labeled "Silver Sirens." Their vessel is docked in a slip that's located in the exclusive isolated part of town known as The Borough. On the table beside their photo lies a yellowing leather-bound book with a silver lock, titled, *The Legend of the Sirens.*

"Who are these Sirens?" I wonder, aloud.

A voice answers from the shadows. "It's best to leave them alone. They were sentenced to life at sea for a reason."

I spin toward the voice. "Lyr! What are you doing sneaking around my property? Never mind that it's six in the morning."

She's dressed in black yoga pants and running shoes. Her face is the color of putty.

"Old folks tend to be morning people," she explains. "At my age, you never know if you will live to see the sunset. You try to get the most out of each day."

"How did you get inside my barn?" I demand. "You need to leave. I know you condemned my mom to death. I don't want to see you again."

She holds up a key. ""I entered through the basement door. This space is owned by the Gray leadership. Check your deed. . It was drafted by a Gray solicitor."

"You're telling me I inherited a house that's not mine?" I flip back my head and laugh. "Does this mean I can't sell the place?"

"Oh, you can sell it, as long as it goes to a Gray."

"Naturally," I jeer, wandering over to the ombudswomans' pictures on the wall. " "Where are the photos of the Gray Wolves and Gray Foxes?"

"They keep them on their respective reservations. They prefer red cedar frames. Their photo rooms smell wonderful."

I move toward the Goddess photos. "Whereas everything about the Gray Goddesses has a nasty stench to it. I point to the wall. "I don't see your picture among the Gray Goddess rank and file, from before you became an Ombudswoman. Were you a Gray Fox? Is your that photo on the Pequot reservation?"

She lifts her nose into the air. "I never had one. I was groomed to be an ombudswoman from the moment I turned. Some women skip the lower phase."

"Speaking of skipping things, Lyr. You've skipped paying your design bill. Though I don't suppose you ever had any intention of paying it."

"Indeed, I did not. I hired you as my interior designer because

I needed to assess your aptitudes. I had to make sure you were nothing like your mother."

I throw up my hands. "Why would you need to assess me? I'm the worst possible choice to become the next Supreme Gray Goddess."

"I quite agree." Lyr backs away from me.

I press in. "Good! Then why can't you and your band of crazy crones leave me alone? You're like crabs in a bucket, trying to keep me from leaving this place."

"Ha! We, Grays, do not hold you here, Snowy. You could have returned to New York right after Slaney's funeral. You found excuses to stay. You wanted to uncover Rebekah's killer. You wanted to sell Slaney's business. You wanted to find Moira. You wanted to accept Zola's job offer. You wanted to capture Kai's affection. Need I go on?" Lyr straightens. "You will always find a reason to remain in Mystick. It's in your blood. Your roots, here, run deep. You are not only a Gray Goddess; you are also a Gray Wolf. Way back, you carry Gray Fox blood, as well. You are a powerful combination of all three, just like me."

I squint at her. "I'm Pequot? You're Mohegan?"

"Remember, Mohegans and Pequots were one tribe, before the colonists arrived. The two split over a disagreement on how to handle the English newcomers. Mohegans moved to the western side of the Thames River and allied with the colonists. Then came that fateful day when the English called upon their Mohegan allies to fight their Pequot relatives, here in Mystick. The colonial soldiers burned down my people's village and murdered our innocent children. That massacre was a dark, hideous, and shameful business."

"I once found a basement mural that depicted those early days in Mystick."

"I know that painting, well. It is also very special to me." Lyr holds her forehead. "It offers a deep time connection to this place."

"Is that why my hair turned gray so young, Lyr? Because of my deep time connection?"

She turns over a picture frame that's facing backwards.

"Mom!" I exclaim.

Lyr fingers Mom's photo like it's poisonous. "Our purpose as Grays is to protect this community against the evils of the 1600s. Once in a great while, someone commits an atrocity that reminds us of those days. It is our duty to punish that person. Rebekah Strangeways was such a person. She met a well-deserved end, after she killed Lucy Wauby."

"*Killed* Lucy Wauby?" My knees weaken. "I knew she kidnapped her. But why would she kill her? Lake Mazeen told me that Rebekah suffered from blind ambition. But I can't see what that has do to with murdering a kid?"'

"I don't order executions lightly, Snowy," qualifies Lyr. "Rebekah not only murdered Lucy, she would have murdered Amani, too, if Riley Finch hadn't hidden her in his shed.

I collapse into a sitting position on the floor. "Riley wasn't kidding when he claimed he was saving Amani from the devil's own? My mom was that devil."

"That's right. We, Grays, couldn't allow her to bring back the darkness of the 1600's. We must never allow the murder of innocent children. Rebekah's execution was an unpleasant necessity. But a necessity, nonetheless. At the time your mother was tried for her crime, she was the most dangerous Gray this town had ever seen. She suffered terribly from the Gray Curse. Her ambition drove her to murder. There was no one she would not harm if it could contribute to her success as a designer. Beware your dark side, Snowy. We, Grays, are creatures of the moon. As Goddesses, Sirens, Foxes, and Wolves, we are drawn to it. It guides our cycles, our power for good or for ill. The moon's dark side calls some Grays more strongly than others. It was a magnet for your mom. Be vigilant against your dark side."

I hold my forehead. "You're telling me to watch my dark side? I never killed anyone or sentenced anyone to death. Execution sounds pretty dark to me. I don't believe Alse approved of Mom's execution. Hell, I don't approve of execution for any reason."

"Alse was sympathetic to Rebekah. You're right about that. She took out Riley's eye for his role in her execution. She struggled with violent tendencies when the Gray Curse infected her. Fortunately, after assaulting Riley, Alse checked into our Gray rehab facility in Brazil. That's how she stopped The Gray Curse from consuming her - as it did your Mom."

"Why didn't you put Rebekah in your rehab facility before she went looney tunes and killed a kid?"

"We wanted to. We tried to. But one of the heralds prevented it by conspiring with her against us."

I examine the photos of the guys in long gray coats. "You mean, one of these guys? Who and what are they? Your henchmen?"

"We prefer to think of them as trusted employees." She points to Manny's photo. "This man fell in with Rebekah's bad crowd and committed a foolish act on her behalf. Since that time, he has worked to make up for that."

"You're talking about Manny Spellman. But if he is a herald, Selkie should have recognized him when he visited her house. She should have recalled seeing him at Gray functions. Or at least remembered seeing him hang out with her baby sister."

Lyr takes a thoughtful pause. "Grays don't notice heralds. We dehumanize them, treat them with the same indignities and pretended invisibility that colonists bestowed upon Native Americans. Dehumanization makes people invisible. We need to clean up our Gray house. The next person who assumes my job, as ombudswoman, will need to address the issue of herald inequality."

I picture Manny's gray vampire coat and pewter space boots. I hit my forehead. "Of course he's a herald. That's why he knew that other herald who pretended to be a homeless person, the guy who was yelling 'Do as you must' from the roof of the Silver Moon on the day of Slaney's funeral. Was that herald there to announce Slaney's passing from the Gray World?"

"No, his name is Summoner. He was there to announce your rise into the Gray World on the day you turned. It's his duty to call out the Rede to new Grays, to remind them of their duty to avoid the Gray Curse."

"Summoner sounds more like a title than a name."

"Heralds take names that describe their functions."

"As would any functionary-cum-minion. What about Manny?"

She starts to hiss and bites her tongue. "He was known as Grayshield because he kept close to the Grays . . . too close, in fact." She presses her lips so tight that they crinkle, finally revealing her antiquity.

"That explains why he tried to cover up Summoner's identity

when we ran into him on the street; he didn't know I'd turned Gray and figured anything concerning the heralds was none of my business." I rocket through more memories of Manny. "There's something else. On the day we met, Manny said, 'Snowy. Love the name. Not the one you were born with.' It struck me as odd that he knew Snowy was not my birth name."

"That's Grayshield, all right, forever trying to get close to the Grays," she sniffs.

I tower over her. "Rebekah is the Gray that Manny got too close to. Isn't he? That closeness explains his dislike of her one-time lover, Clancy O'Connor. It also explains why Manny tried to protect Rebekah even after she fell victim to the Gray Curse."

"You're right. He lost his job as a herald because he got too close to your mom."

My heart pounds like a powwow drum. "There's more, Lyr. Manny's super-tall. Mom's pint-sized. I'm almost six feet. Manny's my dad? Isn't he?"

The light in her eyes fades. I sense that her tenure as ombudswoman is ready to expire.

She inhales with great effort. "Yes, Manny Spellman is your father. Fríða and Slaney hoped you'd never find out. You have much to consider. I will leave you."

"Wait a minute. There's one more thing. Manny is also AWOL. I'd like to speak to his friend, Summoner. I am allowed to speak to him, now that I'm a Gray, aren't I?"

"Indeed, you are. He lives in an apartment over the Silver Moon. Just keep it professional, and be careful. There's no need to repeat your mom's mistakes."

CHAPTER 17
SUMMONER

A busted green rowboat filled with rose geraniums sits by the back door of the Silver Moon Café, along with several recycling bins, a bike rack, and a canary yellow kayak. A pair of gray socks and a gray button-down shirt hang on a clothesline. I'm guessing they belong to Summoner.

I try to lift the wrought iron latch to the back door but it's locked. I hear footsteps coming towards me, from inside, and duck around the side of the house. The door bursts open and out pops a guy my age sloshing a wash bucket. He turns his back to dump his dishwater down a drain. I scurry behind him and up the stairs. Those colonial stairs are old and worn down the middle from centuries of comings and goings, including the troubled footsteps of Cyrus and Rebekah Wright. The door at the top is adorned with a kitsch ceramic face covered with leaves and vines, an image known as The Green Man. A poorly wood-burned plaque below it says, "Summoner."

I knock above the Green Man's head.

The door cracks open.

"You!" squeaks a pale man with starvation eyes. "I'm sorry I ran away from you, before. But Grayshield would have been furious with me, if I . . ."

I pump my palms up and down. "Chill, Summoner. You don't need to hide the fact that you're a herald or that I'm Grayshield's daughter, anymore. I'm a Gray now."

He pulls up his suspenders over a holey, sleeveless tee shirt that says, "Beware My Joystick" and bids me enter. His apartment looks like it belongs to a thirteen-year-old boy. It's covered with comic book posters, half-empty Skittles bags, and scattered video game cases. Two long gray coats hang on wooden pegs on the wall: one is a lightweight duster and the other is made from scratchy winter wool. Both could use a good cleaning. No sheets cover his mattress and his saggy recliner looks like it came from a ghost ship. An outdated television hooked up to a Play-station sits in front of the chair.

Summoner appears transfixed by my appearance. I examine his posters and realize they're mostly fantasy anime girls with stilt legs and razor cut white hair. I stay alert.

"You can play with me, if you like . . . a game, I mean." He points a twitchy finger at his extra game controller.

"Another time," I defer. "There's someone I need to talk to you about."

"Rebekah?" He pulls his shirt up over his mouth. "I hear you're a designer, same as her."

"Not exactly the same. I got rid of the name she gave me so I could be my own person. I understand that you've done the same thing by changing your name to Summoner."

"Yes, ma'am." He snaps his suspenders. "Do you know that I was the one who summoned you?"

"I do. I'm curious, how you knew that I was about to turn."

He snorts with his head down. "Why do you care? Grays don't think us Heralds know anything."

"Summoner," I explain, "I'm a young Gray. I'm open-minded. Tell me how you knew. Cough it up."

He rubs his hands together. "Well, you remember when you drank the seaweed -ea?"

"Yes, it felt like I was drowning in low tide."

"When you drank a full cup," he tee-hees. "I guessed you were a real Gray. Then, of course, those pink spo-s were a dead giveaway." He twitters into his hand.

I put my hands on my hips. "Admittedly, my transformation was a bit ragged."

"Why did you come here?" He gyrates his thumbs, as if he's playing an invisible game controller. "Did I do something wrong?"

I glance at the posters. "Not as far as I know. I'm here to ask if you're the one who summoned my mom when she broke the Rede."

He hunches over, making himself shorter. "I'm afraid so. Tha- was an unhappy summoning day, tha- one."

"My mom suffered from The Gray Curse."

"I'll say!" Summoner points to my tangerine stilettos with a shaking hand. "Her obsession with brigh- colors was the firs- symp- om."

His jumpy eyes keep landing on my shoes. "Please feel free to play one of your games while we talk," I offer. "You look like you need it."

"Thank you." He hops into his seat and grasps the game controller. The stiff wrinkles in his face soften, like he's an addict who just shot up.

"This is your obsession. Isn't it, Summoner?"

"Everybody has one." He presses the buttons and yanks the stick from side to side.

"Yes, they do. The Gray Curse is all about obsession. Right?"

He twitches his shoulders.

"You summoned my mom for violating the Rede. My guess is that her violation had something to do with the colorful kitchen she was working on. Like you said, an obsession with color is the first symptom of the curse." I swallow hard. "What is the second symptom?"

"Killing people," he parrots, like he's answered this a hundred times. His eyes remain focused on the screen, where a star-covered video girl is carrying a giant lollipop while running away from a tongue-wagging hairy monster with bug eyes.

As the monster's tongue flails across the screen, I say, "I have a gut feeling that the Gray Curse also has something to do with the kids who've gone missing."

His eyes remain glued to the screen in front of him. "His eyes remain glued to the screen. "You should ask Grayshield. He's inves-iga-ing the kidnappings."

"You've seen Manny!" I perk up.

"He calls me, now and then," he replies. "He don- like Mystick, because of what happened to your mom. He's searching for the original owner of the gray house near yours. He thinks the owner is connec-ed-o the missing kids. Her name was Bli-ski. She wen- mad after somebody –ook one of her own kids."
was Bli-ski. She wen- mad after one of her own kids was stolen."

"You mean Bliski's child was abducted?"

He holds up a finger, telling me to hold on a second, while he maneuvers the electronic tongue of the monster in his video game around the kid's lollipop and gobbles it down, along with the girl. A hundred gold lollipops fill the screen. His fist pumps the air. He pauses the game and writes on a pad "Blitski!"

"Oh, Blitski, not Bliski."

"Right. Her kid was –aken due to negligence."

"Did Grayshield know this Blitski woman?"

"We all did. But she disappeared as soon as I summoned Rebekah for breaking the Rede."

"Was Blitski summoned for a Gray Curse crime?"

"No. Bu- Grayshield said she should have been. He believed Bliski was the one who killed Lucy Wauby. He said the Grays made Rebekah fry for Bli-ski's crime. Ombudswoman Corby refused to le- us chase Bli-ski. She blamed Rebekah for killing the child in the -runk."

I swoon. "The runk? Do you mean trunk? Lucy was found dead inside a trunk? You don't mean the trunk inside the old mansion that was torn down eight years ago?"

"One and the same. The Grays freaked when they discovered one of their own had killed a child. They did some soul-searching, wondering if they were as bad as the old-time soldiers who killed all those Pequo- kids."

"It's good to hear they still have souls to search," I mutter. "By the Goddess, Summoner, now I know why the police grilled me so hard about how I knew the location of that trunk when I was ten years old."

Summoner starts hyena laughing, as a digital candy kid unhinges its jaw to gobble up his monster. ""Shinola!" he screams, dropping the controller. "I did it!"

Rejuvenated, he says,"Everybody in the whole Gray World knows you found tha- -runk. Some Grays wan-ed me a-summon *you* for murder. But Ombudswoman Corby swore you had no idea there was a dead kid inside."

"She was right. I was there because I simply had to see that mural."

"Yikes." He pokes a swirling finger at me. "Sounds obsessive."

"Maybe so, but it wasn't criminal. I'm not sure the Grays understand their own law very well. What makes them qualified to handle perpetrators of major crimes. Why don't they let the regular police do their job?'

"Usually, they do. The only Gray murderer I know of is your mom."

"Lucky me," I groan.

I step in front of the television and he sits up straight, as if one of his characters jumped out of the screen and came to life.

"Chill, Summoner," I command. "You summoned Rebekah Strangeways because she killed Lucy Wauby due to her obsession with color. But I don't get how her color obsession drove her to murder."

"You should ask a Gray."

"I want you to tell me. Heralds must obey Gray commands. Right?"

He thinks a moment and exhales. "Fine. Rebekah loved Lucy's amazing green eyes. When she discovered the girl wore con-ac- lenses and her eye color was fake, she got angry." He stares at my hair. "You know how the Grays dislike anything unna-ural."

"Sure. But what's that got to do with murder?"

"Af-er Rebekah realized she was fooled by Lucy's fake lenses, Riley overheard her say she was kidnapping Amani Jones because her natural shamrock eye color was perfec- for her ki-chen. Tha-'s why Riley hid tha- Jones girl."

"Of course! Who was Rebekah talking to about killing Lucy?'

"Bli-ski."

"Then Blitski could have been Lucy's killer."

"Tha-s wha- Manny says." He scrunches up his face. "But I dunno."

"Tell me why Mom or Blitski would need to kill pretty girls to find a good room color? Why couldn't Rebekah just copy their eye color for her designs without harming them?"

Summoner rises and twists to maneuver the biggest of the golden lollipops into a slot inside a shining rainbow door. A sparkling number three, for the next game level, flashes on the screen. He pats the joystick , thenturns to me and says, ""The thing with crazy obsessions is they never make sense -o sane people."

I try to picture my mom capturing kids and murdering them. Summoner is right. It doesn't make sense.

"Let me get this straight," I say. "You believe Manny blames Blitski for the murders, because she got in trouble for abusing her own kid."

"Yes. Manny thinks Bli-ski was guilty and no- Rebekah. He also thinks Bli-ski may be responsible for the disappearance of the boy from the Mohegan reservation."

I picture Gertie's panicked expression when River disappeared. I imagine how Zola will freak when she finds out this horrible Blitski woman once owned her house. Maybe she'll sell it and skip town. Then I can buy it and look for clues about Blitski's former crimes against Lucy and Amani and exonerate Mom. Better yet, I'll visit Zola's place, right now, to search for clues.

I'm headed for the heart of The Monster.

CHAPTER 18
DRIP, DRIP, DRIP

Zola's answering machine beeps. "Greetings, Lovely! Sorry to miss you. I'm off shopping for a new home on Ipanema Beach." A chuckle follows. "Just kidding. I'm still in little Mystick, running tiny errands in this microscopic town. The good news is that it won't take long. Leave a message, if you must. I never check this thing."

The snarky bitch is not home, and I don't have a key. But that's not a problem. Curious people learn certain tricks. I slide my credit card into the jam of the old back door that leads to her kitchen. The useless lock pops open on the first try. Breaking in to this home, unbidden, kicks my designing mind into overdrive. I listen carefully, expecting Russ to snarl like a miniature lion. But I hear nothing but a drip, drip, drip sound that turns my stomach. A whiff of something that smells like a sewage leak makes me pinch my nose. Zola must be testing her vile organic milk paints, again. Her eco-friendly habits linger; despite what she says about her new focus on humanity.

The dripping sound stops and I realize I must've imagined it. I peak inside the kitchen and see Mystick Superstition. Nothing remains of Mom's bright green paint, inspired by Lucy Wauby's contact lenses and Amani Jones' natural eye color. Between the cracked army drab glass, the wallpaper featuring black cats, and the ghoulish purple stove and diamond-shaped tile backsplash, I have to say that this is one mediocre kitchen design. What was Zola thinking? What was I thinking? What can I hope to gain by reexamining rooms that have been redone since Mom worked on them?

I peek inside the parlor that Zola promised we'd work on next. Hell on hot rollers!

She's already painted the walls bronze and installed golden brown velvet curtains in the window overlooking the river. How dare she work on this design without consulting me? There's also new furniture in the room that's covered in plastic. I pull off one of the coverings and find a wooden table with a glass cutout in the center that looks like a river, echoing the main hallway floor. It's a gorgeous piece but I'm still steamed. Beneath another plastic cover lies a teal blue and tan striped loveseat and a set of the electric blue velvet chairs. This bitch is designing this whole room on her own. She's ignoring the Snow in Black Snow!

I head toward the stairs, bumping into a maze of paint cans, design boards, fabric samples, and photographs. I wonder what devious designs she has started on the second floor. I head up to Zola's bedroom and find a russet red paint sample slapped on the white wall. I realize it matches the Native American blanket she bought at the Mohegan Wigwam Festival. Screw you, Zola. How dare you do all this design work without consulting me? I need to hire a lawyer to check the details of our partnership contract.

My eyes light up when I notice the bottom drawer of Zola's fabulous Parnian desk is ajar. I peek inside. How many bills has she incurred on my dime without me knowing it? I thumb through the file folders, stuffed with correspondence. I find the envelope with the most recent date—two months old—and open it. A hand-written letter catches my eye

.

Dear Zena,

Your name comes from the Greek god, Zeus. Like Zeus, you like to dominate humanity and wreak havoc on innocents. Like Zeus, you have a secret child. Like Zeus, you pretend to love nature when you are far from earth-friendly. I know that you have been poaching and smuggling endangered plants and animals for years. I obtained surveillance footage of your crimes. I demand that you close your Manhattan office immediately. If you don't, I'll pass on those surveillance records to the media and let the world know that Zola Black and Zena Blitski are the same person.

Earnestly,
W

I collapse into the desk chair. Zola Black is Zena Blitski! How is this possible? No wonder she knew so much about my family. I signed a legal partnership with a smuggler, a phony, and a possible killer. I'm in some serious shit. I've agreed to split everything fifty-fifty with a criminal—including legal fees.

I rifle through another desk file, labeled "Mystick Inspirations." It contains a photo cd. I turn on Zola's PC and try the most likely passwords. Michelangelo. Russ. Lovely. Humanity. Ipanema. Eco-friendly. Black Snow. Wolfie.

No luck.

I dig through wads of paint, wallpaper samples, and find a pile of plastic sleeves filled with printed photographs. The photos show Mystick faces from about a decade ago. I'm startled by a picture of Slaney and Rebekah holding hands with a woman with a wide cleft chin and sharp nose. I flip it over. On the back it says, "Rebekah, Slaney & Zena."

Zena!

This Zena woman looks nothing like Zola. There must be some mistake . . . unless she's had . . . plastic surgery. A deep chill rattles my bones. The copper beech tree that's showing through the window behind the womens' heads is the same tree around which Zola centers her painting ritual. This photo was taken here, inside Monster House.

Wait a minute. How could I be so stupid? If Zola is Zena, she has always owned this house. It was never really up for sale. That means Mom and I both worked with Blitski—Mom on the old bright green kitchen; me on Mystick Superstition. The parallels between me and Mom continue. I picture Mom's head-boxed self-portrait at Granite House, how she felt trapped working with Zola. I sure as hell get that. But I still don't know if the real monster is Mom or Zola. Or both?

I find an overstuffed manila envelope and flip through the photos inside, hoping it contains more information about Zola. The photographs show contemporary people hanging out around the Mystick drawbridge and seaport—biking, walking, and kayaking. They're design study shots for Mystick Picnick. Half the people in town are in these photos. They must be the same faces that Zola used to inspire the images on the toile curtain fabric for Mystick Picnick.

"Fuck humanism!" I shout.

A thump shakes the room. My heart stops. Zola must be home. Did she hear me? I stuff everything back in the drawer and tiptoe into the next room. There's no way I can get down the stairs and out the door without her catching me. I have no way to escape. As always, I hear my nannies saying, "Good God, get a grip girl."

Scoping my surroundings, I spot three pricey armoires that offer three possible hiding places. I can't imagine what Zola is planning to do with these monstrosities. They're as bulky as the case in Lyr's home. But their rare wood finishes are amazing. One is made from an exotic American maple burl, another from Irish Oak Burr, and a third from Nilambur Indian Teakwood. Any decent designer would recognize these endangered woods and stay away from them on ethical grounds. I once sourced the teakwood for a project I was working on at Víðsýni, and Fríða grounded me for a week for a breach of ethics. The Gray Curse is about rampant ambition that makes a person do crazy things. Was my desire to use that prohibited wood an early symptom of The Gray Curse? What was Zola's first symptom? Her obsession with mimicking the magnificent colors and textures of the natural world?

A second thump rips through me. It's coming from close by, real close by—like from inside one of these armoires. I think quickly. The letter said Zola is a poacher. Perhaps one of these armoires contains a bagged spider monkey or chained peregrine falcon that's getting antsy. I open the creaky door of the Irish Oak Burr armoire. There's nothing inside but a pile of cracker crumbs, probably left by a mouse or some other animal. I hear another thump. I throw open the door of the Nilambur Indian Teakwood armoire. Nothing's in here either, except for an empty plastic water bottle. Sweat drips into my eyes, as I approach the American Maple Burl armoire. I fling the door open and jump backwards.

Sunlight illuminates the squinting face of a young boy. He's bound with tasseled curtain tiebacks and gagged with a lemon chiffon window scarf. His gorgeous brown sun-streaked braid sits, snipped off, in his lap. A patch of bronze paint covers his left cheek. A smudge of teal paint under one eye matches his bright blue-green pupils. Several numbered paint swatches are pinned to his neon orange tee shirt.

"By the Goddess. Let me help you!" I say, unbinding the kid.

He chokes out the word, "Parla."

"Don't worry Parla," I say. "I'll get you out of here."

"My name is River," he croaks.

"I know who you are. I was at Mohegan when you disappeared." I give him a light hug. "I'm so glad I found you." I look him over. His droopy eyes suggest he may be tired and hungry but otherwise unhurt.

"I gotta go." He rushes past me to the bathroom. I hear a tinkling sound followed by the mad slurping of water. He steps back out and sputters, "I know you . . . Snowy . . . white-haired Mohegan . . . you . . . help me."

"Yes, I'm Snowy. You're safe, now." I try to mimic Gertie's steady, nurturing, and protective aura. "Do you know if there might be other kids in here, somewhere? Maybe a girl named Moira?"

His speech speeds up. "Dunno. Dunno. Crazy Lady . . . no names . . . only colors . . . inside rooms . . . threes . . . all threes . . . some guy named Michael."

"Michelangelo?" I say.

"Yeah, yeah, him." He squeals, "She wanted me inside the wall, inside Parla." He grabs my shirt, "I'll show you."

I follow him, as he hobbles along on cramped legs, stumbling downstairs to show me that the bronze parlor walls match his skin and the golden-brown velvet curtain fabric is the color of his hair. He points to a teal stripe on the loveseat that matches his eyes. Then he punches the wall near a small section of open sheet rock.

"You see?" he chokes on a sob. "This is for me. It IS me." He bends over and vomits. My hand shakes as I reach to hold his head. He lifts it and speaks, while still gagging. "She was gonna put me inside this wall."

I piece together this grotesque puzzle. Zola wanted her parlor view of the Mystick River to reflect not only the kid's coloring but also this child's essence and physical presence—blood, bones and all. This is the most perverse design peccadillo imaginable.

I hug River, puke splatter and all. "I'll keep you safe," I promise. "You're not going to be trapped behind any walls."

His eyes tear up. "Oh, no! Kitchen girl!" he screams.

"Kitchen girl? Do you mean Moira?" I gasp.

I run to the kitchen and scan the plum stove, olive wallpaper, and diamond backsplash. Nothing here reminds me of Moira. Then a horrible image forms inside my head of a girl with olive eyes, a diamond-shaped face, and eggplant-colored hair. This room mirror's Nahla! But she's with her dad.

River catches up to me.

"This room looks like Nahla Prakesh," I say. "But she's safe with her dad. She must have got away."

He shakes his head. "No! Nobody safe. Crazy Lady spreads lies." He bangs on the walls.

I remember the dripping sound I heard earlier. My heart drops into my feet. What if Nahla is inside these walls? "I bang on the sheetrock, listening for an opening, groping for a break in the wall.

River fingers the walls until he finds the edge of a removable piece of wallpapered sheetrock. I pry it with a heavy kitchen knife and yank it out. Wide olive eyes scream back at me. It's Nahla. Her mouth is duck taped. A puddle lays at her feet and her shorts are soaked. That explains the dripping sound. Her hands are cuffed with plastic ties. I cut the ties with a kitchen knife. Her eggplant hair is matted and her olive skin looks gray. But she's still alive.

I pull her out and hold her shivering body. River staggers to fetch her a cup of water, spilling half of it.

"You're safe now, Kitchen," mumbles River, vibrating. "I was Parla.' He grabs a big towel from the bathroom and wraps her damp legs in it.

"Who are you?" Nahla asks, frightened of me.

"I'm here to stop Crazy Lady," I reply.

"I want my mom and dad . . . why didn't they come?" whimpers Nahla.

River pats her shoulder. "Crazy Lady sent your mom fifty thousand dollars, and pretended it came from your dad."

His words feel like a sledge hammer to my chest. "No, River. Crazy Lady didn't bribe Nahla's mom. You're talking about Moira O'Connor's mom. That money went to her."

Nahla shrieks "My Moira! Dining Room! Oh no! Selfish me! Forgot my best friend!" She moans from deep inside.

I rush to the dining room. The kids slog along as best they can.

My head shakes at the sight of those incredible toile curtains printed with Mystick faces in soft reds and greens. For the first time, I notice the image of a girl with boiled lobster hair and seagrass eyes, just like the colors of Mystick Picnick. What a fool I've been.

"It's Moira!" I scream. "How did I not notice her before? How?"

I feel around for the opening. "We need to find her. She could be anywhere," I tell Nahla and River.

Nahla is heaving mournful sobs. I know I should be comforting her. But there's no time. My mind reels, trying to process the fact that Zola used children to inspire her designs and then sealed them in the walls of her interiors. I understand why Summoner was so freaked out by me. He summoned my mom for stealing Lucy's coloring and sealing her in a trunk. He figured that anyone who did that was a real monster. He was right.

I picture the photo I found of Mom with Zola and try to piece things together. Did Mom plan to put Amani inside a wall? Or was it Zola who plotted to trap the girl, all along?

"Hustle kids!" I shout.

The kids push themselves.

"Here!" squeals Nahla. "Help . . . her."

I hear a click.

A small section of sheetrock breaks off. Through it, I spot a cat's paw birthmark on pink flesh. I tear open more of the wall and find a floppy head covered in lobster red hair. I peel the rest of the sheet rock away and grab Moira. She's slumped against the wall, not moving. I push her hair away. Her eyes are closed.

"No!" shrieks Nahla.

I grab Moira's arms and hold her. She's limp. River runs for a glass of water. I press it to her lips. Her eyes flutter as she drinks. Her nails dig into me. Nahla squeals. I carry Moira to the bathroom and grab another towel. Her cotton skirt is covered with stains.

River peeks out the window. "Somebody's coming! What do we do?"

"It's Crazy Lady! chokes Nahla.

Moira stares at me in silent dread.

"What do we do?" River clenches his teeth.

"I'm a Gray," I say boldly. "I fight the dark tides. I will protect you."

"Or you'll become a black and white bathroom," Nahla whispers.

"Never," I say, hugging her. "Never again will anyone be trapped inside these walls."

River garners the courage to peek outside. "It's a man," he says. "He could be working with her."

A voice from outdoors yells, "Snowy!"

The kids' eyes question me.

"Don't worry," I say, recognizing the voice. "It's my friend Kai. He'll help us."

River and Nahla drag themselves outside. I carry Moira, who still hasn't spoken.

"What the-," says Kai, stepping away from his Land Rover. "What are you doing with the missing kids?"

"Zola kidnapped them."

"Oh, man." He pats their shoulders. "I'm glad you're all okay."

"I was Parla," mumbles River. "This white-haired Indian girl saved me."

"Parla? What's he saying?" Kai asks me.

"River was scheduled to go inside the parlor walls." I explain, choking on a sob. "Zola used these kids as inspiration for her room designs, and then planned to seal them in those rooms. Moira was sealed behind the dining room wall when we found her; Nahla was trapped behind a kitchen wall. They all need to see a doctor."   "What   the f-? She sealed kids behind walls to enhance her designs? No way. That's some freaky black magic." He whispers in my ear, "What did she plan to do about their decomposing bodies?"

I whisper back, "My guess is she was planning to leave town for a few years to let the place air out, once she finished the parlor. It's not the first time she's skipped town. She did something similar under her old name of Zena Blitski."

"Zola is Zena? The woman who lived here years ago? The one who lost custody of her kid? But she didn't look like . . ."

I point to my face. "Surgery. I should have figured out that there was something wrong with Zola. When she bought this house, she told me it would reflect the true beauty of humanity. She meant that literally. Rebekah Strangeways may have helped Zola steal Lucy and try to steal Amani. But Zola took it to the next level by putting kids inside walls."

Kai checks out every car whizzing down River Road. "We need to get these kids the hell out of here, Snowy. Zola could return at any moment."

"Let's go to my aunt Selkie's place. It's right down the street. I can call an ambulance from there."

"Right," says Kai. "We need to move fast."

"After I drop you guys off," he says, "I'm heading straight back here. If she arrives before the cops and finds the kids gone, she may bolt. I'm won't let that happen. And Snowy: the Grays need to deal with her as soon as possible. No more kids can suffer because of this monster."

PART IV
FINDING CEDAR

CHAPTER 19
DARK TIDES

Gertie heaves open the accordion-style partition at the back of the *Mystick Lights* newsroom, exposing a crowded room the size of a gymnasium. A cloud of sage wafts my way.

"The Great Gray Hall welcomes you," she announces.

My gut churns. Having just discovered kids stuffed behind the walls of Monster House, this Gray habit of personifying buildings sickens me.

Grays cluster around the walls that abut other downtown buildings. The wall opposite me contains three portal windows that overlook the river. Through them, I spy a yacht filled with waving women that I presume are The Silver Sirens. Bookending the porthole windows are watercolor paintings of the Celtic Goddesses—Arianrhod of the moon, Cerridwen of the cauldron, Macha of the crow, along with a Native American painting of a fox staring up at Grandmother Moon. A half dozen heralds hang out in the corners, trying to stay invisible— except for Riley. He stands in the center, beneath the large round lighting fixture that is painted like the surface of the moon. He's petting Barnacle's black fur, as though the cat is the reincarnation of Slaney, taking her rightful place at the center of the Mystick Gray world. Riley is the only herald who is carrying a cat; but plenty of the Grays are holding them, and they lend a soothing purring sound to the gathering.

The cliques stand out: Foxes hang with Foxes, Wolves with Wolves, and Goddesses with Goddesses. These women have been at peace since the Pequot Massacre of 1637 but they're still not fast friends. Gertie stands at the center of the Gray Wolves, wearing shapeless black pants with a red silk blouse that does nothing for her lumpy figure. She's accessorized it with dangly beade feather earrings and low black pumps. Edith huddles with the Gray Foxes, resplendent in a beaded wampum collar, serious metallic heels, and a stunning lavender sheath that was either purchased out-of-town or at one of Foxwoods Casino's high-end shops. All the Native Americans in attendance wear some sort of beaded jewelry, like it's their tribal membership card. None of them sports ceremonial clothing. Gray meetings are separate from their tribal ceremonial life. For them, these gatherings represent an ongoing diplomatic peacekeeping mission with the newcomers.

For the Gray Goddesses, this room offers the only safe community space where they can practice their Celtic spirituality and other European divine female goddess traditions. Their regalia includes fabulous pendants, wide hemp belts, and hooded flax robes, similar to the ones in the watercolor portraits of their iconic goddesses on the far wall. I move to check out those paintings and see they are all signed "S. Strangeways," with the letter "S" drawn like a mermaid. *Nice job, grandma.* The luminous grandmother moon painting that includes a fox is signed E.W. "Moon Dancer." That's got to be Edith. I had no idea she was such a masterful painter.

I catch my reflection in one of the windows that overlooks the docks. Oh, hell on hot rollers! I'm a bloody mess! My hair looks like a dirty snowball. My Mohegan wolf tee shirt is stained with I–don't-want-to-know-what. I examine my chipped nails. The girls at Hips would say I look like a skid row hooker. But it doesn't matter. I can't change or rest until I hear that Kai succeeded in helping Police Chief Lara Oakley apprehend child serial killer Zola Black.

This has been a day like no other. My morning began by finding Lyr in my barn basement, where I learned she executed Mom for murder and that Manny was my dad. Then I met the herald, Summoner, and found out Dad was hunting Zena Blitski, who turned out to be Zola Black, my next-door neighbor and business partner. After that, I discovered the missing kids at Monster House and learned that mom's former design partner, i.e. my current partner, was using them as macabre muses, sealing them into the walls of the newly designed rooms in her house. Another wave of nausea comes over me.

Gertie smooths my messy hair. "It will be all right," she consoles.

I grab her hand. "Considering what's happened, I expected everyone to ply me with questions the moment I arrive."

"It's our Gray custom to allow one another time to gather their thoughts, before our gatherings commence. It centers us." She winks. "It also prevent arguments from starting before our meetings have a chance to begin."

I check the clock. An hour has passed since I rescued Moira, Nahla, and River from Monster House. Kai's still-precarious situation at that location worries me. But the Gray Goddesses, Gray Foxes, Gray Wolves, and Gray Sirens could not have convened this emergency meeting any faster. Wolves and Foxes had to drive from their respective reservations. Goddesses had to ride their bikes or kayak from different parts of Mystick. Sirens had to sail in from The Borough.

Except for the Sirens, each of the local Gray groups is represented in the décor of this hall. A backdrop of crushed purple and white quahog shells covers the wall on the right. Those shells reflect the Foxes and Wolves' belief in the protective and cleansing power of wampum, just as Slaney's portraits reflect the Goddesses' belief in the healing power of their legendary goddesses. Beside the podium stands a carved wolf. The initials GM are carved into it. And here I had no idea that Gertie was a skilled carver.

A weathered oak seal, depicting three women holding hands in a circle, hangs on the opposite wall. Two of these historic women figures are dressed in buckskin. The one in seventeenth century Irish clothing is Rebekah Wright. The seal is bounded by a circle of carved waves. Inside that circle are the words Aquya/Peace – Missituck/Mystick – Corn Planting Moon, May, 1637.

Alse enters the room with her back bowed, feeling the weight of recent Gray matters,. Her gossamer Gray Goddess formalwear makes her look like a glamorous ghost. Its shimmering silver color represents the bright light of the full moon that illuminates justice.

My eyes are drawn back to the painting of Cerridwen, Goddess of the Cauldron that is supposed to contain wisdom. I look deep into that cauldron for guidance on how to understand a woman who stole children to inspire interior designs and then tried to murder them so her house would "reflect the true beauty of humanity."

Lyr taps my shoulder She's wearing a charcoal gray judge's robe, beaded with rows of tubular purple and white wampum at the neck and cuffs.

"Were you thinking of Cerridwen when you designed the cauldron for Mystick Superstition?" she asks.

My response sticks inside my throat, as I picture the kitchen at Monster House and remember the moment I found a little girl with olive eyes and eggplant hair shut behind a wall.

Lyr drops her head into her hands. "I'm so sorry. It was foolish of me to bring up that kitchen. It was also foolish of me to get into a spat with you, earlier. I was agitated for personal reasons." She tries to straighten but her posture is still poorer than usual. "Gertie tells me a lot has happened since I saw you this morning. You saved the lives of three children. You've been through a great deal. Look into Cerridwen's eyes. There, you'll find a blessing, left for you by your Grandma Slaney. It's the perfect time for you to receive it."

I examine Cerridwen's eyes and speak dreamily. "There's a cedar sprig in Cerridwen's eyes, like the silver moons painted in Rebekah Wright's eyes. Did Slaney paint this cedar for me?"

Lyr brings her hands to her heart. "Absolutely. It honors your birth name of Cedar Strangeways. As you know, cedar is the strongest of our Native cleansing plants." She catches her breath. "Indeed, we, Grays, need that cedar cleansing today."

"It's funny," I say. "I always thought Moira was her favorite, that all she cared about was preparing Moira to replace her. I admit that I was jealous. Now I see how much Slaney also cared for me. I was so afraid when I did not find Moira, right away. I had to nearly lose her to realize how much I care for that little girl."

Lyr squeezes my hand. "Having a Gray perspective on the world changes things. In local Native tradition, we use the word grandmother for any wise woman who cares for her people. You, my dear, have shown yourself to be a fine, nurturing grandmother. Slaney knew you were destined for great things. That's why she provided you with a sophisticated Gray upbringing, sending you to live with Fríða—the most powerful ombudswoman in this country."

"What?" Her words rattle me. "You're saying that Fríða Olafsdottir is the Gray Ombudswoman of New York City? No way."

She lowers her wrinkled eyelids. "I'm surprised you didn't know. When the New York Gray Apples made female gender self-identifying a decade ago, Fríða joined the Gray Goddesses. She skyrocketed up the ranks to become ombudswoman. The number of Gray Apples has doubled under her leadership."

The Grays begin moving toward the walls. Riley retreats to join his fellow heralds, in the corners. Lyr, Edith, Gertie, and Alse step into the newly-vacated center space and beckon me to join them, beneath the central moon globe. Close up, the subtle gray and tan shading of the craters catch my eye. Slaney must have painted this moon. I'm beginning to appreciate the beautiful banality of her plain New England palate in a town where bad things happen if you get too colorful. Alse shakes a rattle made of mussel shells. Edith shakes a gourd rattle with a fox on it, and Gertie shakes one with a wolf.

The four Gray leaders in the room raise their arms.

"We call this Gray gathering to order," they say, in unison.

All conversation halts.

"As you know, your Gray leaders have called this meeting to put forth a serious accusation," declares Edith.

"I call on Snowy Strangeways to deliver it," states Gertie.

"What!" blurts out Nori Moon, stepping into the center. "Why is that girl speaking instead of one of our Gray leaders?"

"Because Nori," says Gertie, "as you will soon discover, we have failed you." "

"Gertie is right. We do not deserve to tell this tale," adds Alse. She clears her throat and turns her back on Nori to address the rest of the assemblage. "For those Grays who have recently turned, allow me to explain our process. When one of our members determines that a crime has been committed that may "cross the line"—according to the Native Gray *Qutuhikan*—or cause harm according to the Rede, we gather and hear that claim. In the case of a guilty verdict in the worst capital crimes, the ombudswoman may call for capital punishment."

"Execution is medieval!" shouts one of the younger Gray Goddesses.

"Agreed," responds Alse. "That sentence is issued only when a mortal crime strikes at the core of our founding principles. That's why all Grays suffering from Gray Curse issues must make a mandatory visit to our Brazilian rehabilitation facility, to avoid falling victim to the worst aspects of the curse that invoke capital crimes. Any Gray capital crimes that are attempted but not carried out result in lifetime imprisonment at sea. Those thus convicted become Silver Sirens. The incarcerated Sirens still enjoy some Gray privileges, including the right to vote on cases such as this one."

"Please step under the moon, Snowy," instructs Gertie.

My eyes drift up to that moon—symbol of the celestial grandmother that watches over all of us. I think of her grandchildren, trapped behind those walls. I wonder who could be worthier of capital punishment than a person who would do something like that?

"Snowy, please tell us what you discovered today and how you came upon it," prods Gertie.

As I step forward, I feel the heavy burden of speaking for River Mazeen, Nahla Prakesh, and Moira O'Connor.

"Greetings fellow Grays," I gesture towards the river. "*Rivers know all things—past, present, and future. Flowing like time, they are endlessly cleansing, with occasional ripples of dark tides. We Grays stand as a force of light against those dark tides, maintaining the balance, living in the shades of gray.*"

A few Grays snort at my trite words. Most appear surprised.

"I recited this ancient verse because it relates to the difficult issue now facing us. Today, I visited the herald you know as Summoner. Our conversation led me to believe there might be clues to the whereabouts of the missing local children at the house next door to mine on River Road, a house that once belonged to Zena Blitski. As many of you know—and as I only recently discovered—my mother, Rebekah Strangeways, was designing the interiors of her house when she succumbed to the Gray Curse and murdered young Lucy Wauby." I lower my head in regret. "Because my mom worked with Zena, I wondered about Zena's possible culpability in that murder, as well as herconnection to the recent child abductions. So I broke into Zena's old house, hoping to find evidence."

"Breaking and entering. Typical Strangeways' behavior," blurts out Nori.

"Listen Nori," I say. "This time, my crazy curiosity saved lives. I found evidence that Zola Black and Zena Blitski are the same person."

A hissing sound fills the room.

"What's worse, I found three kidnapped children. Moira O'Connor and Nahla Prakesh were trapped behind the walls. River Mazeen was stuffed inside a closet."

Grays shout, demanding answers.

"Are the kids all right?"

"Who did this?"

"The villain must be punished."

Gertie chimes in, "The children are all safe and well—thanks to Snowy."

The room settles down to a feline purr with a few snarls.

I try to look some of the skeptical Grays in the eye. "These kids—Nahla, Moira, and River— told me that Zola, or rather Zena, used their skin, hair and eye coloring as inspiration for her room designs. When she finished creating her human-inspired interiors, she enclosed the children inside three armoires. When she was nearly ready to leave town, she began moving them into the walls of the rooms she designed to enliven them. River Mazeen was still trapped inside his armoire, awaiting transfer to the walls, when I found him. Nahla and Moira were already sealed inside the walls of the house.

Loud hissing erupts, turning the room into a gigantic snake pit.

"Are you saying Zola used these kids like spirited paint to enhance her designs?" asks Edith. "Isn't that what your mother did with poor Lucy?"

"Yes," I sniffle.

"How did Zola manage all this on her own?" asks Edith.

"My best guess is that she flattered Moira and Nahla's dads to find out when they planned to dump their wives and leave town. The she knew when to steal their kids to throw suspicion on the missing dads. With River, she was too rushed to carry out such an elaborate plan."

I step towards Riley and pet Barnacle. Riley gives me a quizzical look. The cat nuzzles my arm with his head, and I feel a chill. "Oh no! I just remembered something." I move away from the cat, recalling Zola's words about cat's being human familiars, at their master's beck and call. A dizzy feeling comes over me, and I reveal, "The coloring of Zola's Somali kitten, Russ, matches her bedroom walls. By the Goddess! I'm afraid she may have hidden him in her walls. Please, someone go look for that cat, right away."

Several Grays screech, in horror. Alse directs two heralds to head over to Monster House. I fear that my recent focus on humanism and humanity made me overlook this serious non-human crime.

"That poor kitten." Alse raps her cane on the floor. "This is my fault," she says. "I should have recognized Zola as Zena. But I am an old woman, and I was flattered by her attentions at Slaney Strangeways's funeral. Now I see that hideous creature was only stalking our children. I apologize to this esteemed group for my foolhardy selfish actions."

Gertie takes Alse's hand and hangs her own head. "Zola also fooled me."

"Where is Zola now?" asks Edith, grinding her teeth.

"Kai Corby asked Lara Oakley to meet him at Zola's house. They're waiting there, to apprehend her, when she shows up," I explain.

Edith's brow furrows. "What's that young man got to do with our Gray business?"

"Kai had been looking for me at Mermaid Cottage. When he didn't find me there, he went next door to Zola's place. He showed up just as I was leaving with the kids. Once I told him what had happened, he drove us to Selkie O'Connor's house and offered to return to Zola's place, in case she came home before Lara and the police arrived."

"Kai is an honorable young man, so that's logical," says Nori. "However, Snowy, it's equally logical to suppose that you already knew what Zola was doing with those kids, as you were involved in planning the room designs which she kidnapped them to enhance. How do we know Kai didn't catch you in the act of helping Zola do something horrible to those kids?"

"That is a reasonable question, considering your pedigree, Snowy," notes Edith.

Gertie responds for me. "The abducted children can answer any questions you have about Snowy's activities, once they've had a change to rest." says Gertie. "For now, Snowy is not the one whose criminal actions we are gathered to consider."

"I smell another cover-up," Nori holds her nose.

"Manny Spellman must have something to do with all this," mutters Alse, eyes flaring. "He's probably working with Rebekah's old friend, Zena, Zola, or whatever she calls herself these days."

"No way," I correct her. "Manny hated Zena. When she hired him to investigate Moira's case, he was fooled by her new face and new identity as Zola. She was able to play him, leaking a photo of Police Chief Lara Oakley kissing Clancy O'Connor to suggest a romantic conspiracy as motive for Moira O'Connor's kidnapping. He fell for anything that made Lara and Clancy—aka Rebekah's executioner and ex-lover— look bad."

A rash of hissing follows this statement, but I keep talking. "Zola led Manny to believe Clancy and Lara also kidnapped Moira's best friend, Nahla. To cement suspicion on Clancy, Zola sent fifty thousand dollars to Moira's mom, Selkie, pretending it was blood money from Clancy, for the theft of their child."

Nori pipes up, again. "We all know Manny wanted to condemn Lara because she executed his girlfriend, Rebekah, for killing Lucy Wauby. But I would like to remind my fellow Grays that Snowy Strangeways was caught red-handed near the trunk that contained Lucy's body. I wouldn't be surprised if Snowy was an accessory to Lucy's murder, despite her young age. She was a very mature child." She looks me up and down, disdainfully. "She still is. I find it a bit too coincidental that she always appears at the location where our kidnapped children are found."

Lyr steps forward in her imposing judge's robe. "Enough, Nori. We concluded long ago that Rebekah killed Lucy. Snowy had nothing to do with it. Neither did Zola."

"I'm still not convinced we've heard the whole story," Nori hisses. "Why did Zola wait until she had taken three kids to put them inside the walls?"

Gertie speaks up, "Snowy, do you have an answer to that?"

"I think so," I say between my teeth. "Zola is obsessed with the number three, due to her love of Michelangelo. He considered the number charmed. Until she abducted a third child, it's possible she felt she couldn't imbue her designs with enough enchantment. Once she took that third child and sealed them all inside her house, she believed her designs would reflect 'the true beauty of humanity.' Once she returned, I presume she planned to disappear for a few years while the kidnapping cases grew cold and the children's bodies decomposed."

The room fills with groans.

Nori steps in front of me, sporting a cool Cheshire Cat grin. "Let me get this straight: the third child she abducted was a Mohegan boy. And she took that boy after you accompanied her to the Mohegan Reservation. Yet we're supposed to believe that was just another coincidence? Isn't it more likely that you were in on Zola's plan, all along? Or worse, that you were its originator, just like your Mom?"

Nori's fans hiss in support.

"Hold it right there, Nori," I slash. "I went to Mohegan to find out more about my heritage. I had no idea that I was speeding up Zola's dark process by allowing her to get close to River Mazeen."

A herald calls Lyr away, explaining that she has an important phone call from Lara. Everyone strains to listen in but the person on the other end is doing all the talking. I can hardly breathe, waiting to hear the news. My heart pounds as Lyr nods into the telephone.

She hangs up and says, "Lara Oakley just called to inform me that the alleged criminal, Zola Black, is now in her custody."

My ears shatter from the cheers.

CHAPTER 20
SECRET SON

Lara Oakley drags herself into the Great Gray Hall. This is not the heroic monster slayer we cheered, a half hour ago. She motions Edith, Gertie, Lyr, and Alse to join her in a private huddle. They wave me in, as well.

After Lara recounts her story, Edith fumes loud enough for everyone to hear, "How could you allow the prisoner to escape?"

"I don't know how it happened," Lara replies to the stunned gathering. "One minute Zola was cuffed in the back of my police cruiser, the next minute, she was gone."

I feel my legs buckle beneath me and whisper, "Where is Kai?"

No one seems to hear me.

Edith booms, "Lara Oakley, you've arrested two major Gray criminals in your career as Mystick Police Chief, and you've lost both of them!"

"What is she talking about?" I ask Gertie.

"Your mom also escaped from Lara, Snowy. Manny helped her slip away because he thought she was innocent."

"Was she innocent?" My heart heaves with hope.

"Not remotely," says Gertie, shaking her head. "I would have helped her escape, myself, if I had any doubt. As it was, all I could do was turn over her clogs to protect her spirit. Even Slaney supported Rebekah's harsh sentence, once she realized what her daughter had done to Lucy. Remember, Lucy was a Pequot, and the Grays were forged in the flames of the Pequot Massacre. Slaney was a descendant of those torch-bearing colonists, just as Edith is a descendant of the massacred Pequots, just as Rebekah descended from the Mohegans who allied with the colonists and watched that horrible violence play out. We, Grays, had no choice but to make Rebekah pay the ultimate price."

Gertie takes my hands, "Once Rebekah escaped custody, your parents ran to Mermaid Cottage to grab what little money she'd stashed away. But the heralds caught them. Lara executed Rebekah on the spot with Riley's help, per Lyr's instructions. Unfortunately, you came home early. There was no time to clean up your mom's execution scene before you arrived. I'm so sorry you had to see all that blood."

"All that blood," I say, vibrating. "Everything you, Grays, do is about blood. It's either about doing penance for the blood of the ancestors, or avenging someone's blood, or continuing the bloodlines that carry on Gray traditions. You live in the Dark Ages. I can't believe you think it's okay to execute people."

"Not people," Edith steps in, holding up a single finger. "One person, Snowy. We have executed one woman in four hundred years. She just happened to be your mom. We tried to stop her before she went too far. But we failed Rebekah. More importantly, we failed Lucy Wauby. Please try and imagine that Rebekah wasn't your mom. Then consider how you might feel."

"Execution is barbaric!" I shout. "Plenty of Grays agree with me on this."

Dozens of women raise their hands in affirmation.

"It's natural you wouldn't want to see your mom harmed, regardless of her actions," says Nori. "But maybe you shouldn't be so forgiving. Rebekah's actions also harmed you. When you were a kid, I was forced to print stories in *Mystick Lights*, suggesting that you killed Rebekah, to hide her Gray execution from the general public. I knew there was no evidence against you. I hoped those articles would be enough to make you shut up and drop the issue. But you insisted on uncovering the whole truth. That's why Slaney sent you away to live with Fríða. It was for your own good. If you'd had a chance, I'm sure you would've tried to help your mom escape custody just like your dad did. A child will do anything for a parent."

Nori's words jangle like loose change inside my mind.

I repeat them out loud. "*A child will do anything for a parent.* Wait a minute, Nori," I say. "I found a letter at Zola's house, claiming she had a child. Maybe that child—who is an adult by now—was the one who helped Zola escape from Lara."

Lyr rolls her eyes to the ceiling, as if calculating something. "The math doesn't work. Kai is twenty-two. Zola is sixty-eight. Who has a baby at forty-six?"

"A rich woman who is willing to pay big money for fertility treatments, that's who," grumbles Edith.

"I suppose it's possible," admits Lyr.

Lara joins in, "Your idea is still a bit far-fetched, Snowy. What makes you think that's what happened?"

""Something in my gut. Were you with Kai and Zola the entire time, Lara? Or did they have a chance to speak, alone?"

Her voice quavers. "I trusted he'd keep an eye on her while I took some crime scene photos inside the house. When I came back out, Zola was gone. Kai wasn't in the car, either. He exited the house house moments later, claiming he had to use the bathroom.."

' "Then let's question him right now!" I say.

"We can't," counters Lara. "He had to leave town, to complete some investigative assignment for *Mystick Lights*."

"I didn't assign him anything," contradicts Nori.

Lyr addresses her. "Then maybe he just wanted to get out of town due to his recent breakup with Brook Beemer. Claiming Kai is Zola's kid is pretty far-fetched."

I face Lyr, whose eyeliner seems to be running. "Is it, now? You once suggested to me that Kai's birth mom was a dangerous woman. Zola showed keen interest in Kai. She gave him the news scoop on our partnership. She also hugged him a bit too warmly at our open house. Is Kai Zola's son?"

Lyr pulls a tissue from her sleeve and wipes her damp eyes. "Snowy, you once told me that a good designer considers all the possibilities, and you have done that. Yes, Zola is Kai's biological mother. His birth name was Zenger Blitski."

I slap my forehead, in recognition. "After the great journalist, John Peter Zenger."

Confusion erupts. Gertie, Alse, and Edith raise their arms to quiet the Grays.

Edith's fists fly into the air. "I can't believe this, Lyr! As our ombudswoman and a Pequot woman, you know this adoption information should have been disclosed."

Lyr raises two protective palms. "I'm sorry, Edith. I swore that I would never disclose anything."

Edith hovers over Lyr. "You swore? Swore to whom? A murderer? Three children nearly died because of your treacherous secret. Tell your Gray sisters the details of Kai's adoption, right now."

Grays from all three groups move in and circle Lyr.

She takes a stilted breath before responding. "Zena Blitski, also known as Zola Black, lost custody of Kai, or rather Zenger, after an unfortunate accident. When he was a baby, his parents had been partying and his dad threatened Zena with a knife. Zena lunged at Kai's dad to grab it away, but he fell and sliced Kai's nose down the middle. Zena rushed Kai to the hospital. His dad took off on them. Kai was left with a permanent nose scar. Social services found drugs at the family's home. His mom lost custody of Kai. I offered to become Kai's guardian so he wouldn't go to a stranger."

She chokes on a sob. "I know I was being selfish by keeping this secret. But I wanted a child, and ombudswomen can't birth children or have them living in Granite House. That's why I built a separate dwelling for Kai. Zena let me adopt him, on the condition that I never exposed his real parentage. I spoke up now about the adoption because she broke the law."

"You spoke up now because you got caught," says Edith. "This is shameful behavior for an ombudswoman."

Lyr sobs. "You're right, Edith. Snowy is also right. Zola probably revealed her maternity to Kai so he would try to save her. Sadly, I was no better a mom to him than she was. I condemned Kai to a loveless childhood in a lonely, isolated granite prison. Zola wrote me letters saying she was going mad seeing other peoples' children living happy lives and wanted a kid around her house to love and admire. That's why she decided to take a chance on plastic surgery and change her name; so, she could return to town and visit Kai. But along with her new name and good looks came unexpected career success. Success consumed her. It delayed her return to Mystick. Meanwhile, Kai grew up. Yet she still felt the emptiness. She got so desperate to have beautiful children in her house that her maternal need turned dark and deranged. That's why she began taking kids and . . ."

"Stop!" Gertie is shaking from head to toe. "Do not make excuses for that killer. You've got me wondering if your adoption of Kai made you vulnerable to blackmail. Did you falsely convict Rebekah Strangeways, eight years ago? Is Zola the one who killed Lucy Wauby? Was Rebekah innocent?"

Lyr Corby looks as though she is about to faint. "No." She turns to me. "I swear that Rebekah was guilty."

"Yet you still failed to disclose your bias in the case," qualifies Edith.

Lyr cowers. "Indeed, that is true. I hereby offer my resignation as Gray Ombudswoman."

Edith shouts, "All in favor of accepting Lyr's resignation, please raise your hands."

Every Gray hand in the room flies into the air, including mine.

"I propose that Lyr Corby be remanded to our Gray rehab facility in Brazil," states Edith. "Does our Gray leadership agree?"

Alse and Gertie nod.

"Heralds!" calls Edith, "Please confirm that Supreme Silver Siren Mab Kincaid and the Sirens are also in agreement with this order."

A hot young herald with a crow neck tattoo dashes off to the dock. I see how Mom fell for one of these bad boys. He returns in less than a minute with his thumbs up.

"Heralds!" calls Edith. "Please remove Lyr Corby and make arrangements for her transport to our facility in Brazil."

The young herald carts her away.

Edith speaks up. "Fellow Grays, we must vote on a replacement for Lyr."

Gertie jumps in. "I recommend that Snowy Strangeways serve as Lyr's replacement. She was raised by New York City Ombudswoman Fríða Olafsdottir, and the late Mystick Supreme Gray Goddess, Slaney Strangeways. Lyr already affirmed her suitability. She solved this most recent case involving The Gray Curse."

Gertie's pronouncement feels more like a harpoon to my chest than an honor.

"You've got to be kidding!" hollers Nori. "We're supposed to take Lyr's recommendation? If Snowy's so smart, why didn't she figure out what her own partner was doing to our kids, before it was nearly too late?"

Gertie talks over her, "Nori, Snowy is not your enemy. All in favor of Snowy as our new Gray Ombudswoman?"

"Just a moment, Gertie!" Nori inserts. "Snowy is your grand-niece. The girl already takes after your wicked niece, Rebekah, in her choice of a career and a business partner. Just look at her! Picture her shorter with her natural hair color and you will remember the monster who bore her." Nori walks around the room. "Have you all lost your minds and forgotten what Rebekah did? Rebekah Strangeways murdered Lucy Wauby. She didn't stick her in a wall. But she did stuff her inside a trunk."

"You need to let go of your prejudices against the Strangeways, Nori," directs Gertie.

"I'm not prejudging anything." She points at me. "Lara and her officers caught Snowy red-handed, trying to pry open that trunk eight years ago. That's suspicious. I refuse to believe she didn't know her partner took the three kids for her interior designs."

"Listen, Nori, "I say. "I didn't expect the Grays to offer me this leadership position." I turn to the group. "I realize that many of you are picturing me with toad brown hair, just like the legendary storybook villain, Rebekah Strangeways. But I assure you, I am nothing like her. What's more,I never expected you to conduct a witch-hunt against me."

The minute I used the "w" word, I regretted it. But oddly, it seemed to make more Gray faces appear sympathetic.

Supreme Gray Fox Edith Wyouggs narrows her upturned eyes, revealing deep distress. "Snowy," she says, "I attended the failed ceremonies to heal your mom. I would like to think you don't take after her. But it is my duty as Supreme Gray Fox and a Pequot woman to be careful about who we, Grays, choose as ombudswoman. Justice is required to maintain peace, which is our primary Gray goal. Safeguarding that justice is the ombudswoman's mission. I know you were taught solid Gray values by our illustrious New York Ombudswoman and the late Supreme Gray Goddess of Mystick. But you carry the same face as the most violent Gray we have ever known. I am hopeful that face is only a mask. However, the Grays were founded in reaction to the violence of English colonists against my Pequot people with the consent of your Mohegan Tribe. So naturally, I'm skeptical about Mohegans with violent family tendencies."

"Here! Here!" hollers Nori. "I'm with you, Edith. Many of us are wary of Snowy. I therefore ask that you consider me as an alternate candidate for ombudswoman. I have always protected the Grays with my articles in *Mystick Lights*. I have years of experience, and there is no tarnish upon my family name or record."

"No way!" shouts someone at the back of the room. A spiked head of hair with a gray streak pushes through the crowd. "Please make way," says a familiar voice. A young Gray in low-riding cargo shorts and a khaki vest with a gazillion pockets moves to the center of the room.

"Lightning," I breathe.

She winks at me. "Hi, everybody. I'm new here. My name is Lightning. I just became a Gray Wolf, this year, and I've already stepped into the middle of a slippery mess. That's a habit of mine." She points to the ace bandage on her still-healing leg, and a few people chuckle.

"Anyway," she says. "I witnessed an argument between Lyr and Nori that relates to the issue at hand."

Conversation rises like a tidal wave. All of the Grays point and mutter about this odd Mohegan teen.

"Please tell us a little about yourself, Lightning," sniffs Edith. "I've heard you dabble in some of our old medicine."

"That is true, Edith. But mostly I just study architecture at RISD."

A group of the younger Grays chuckle.

Lightning continues, "Right now, I'm balancing two summer jobs. I wait tables at The Silver Moon and work as a security guard at Mohegan Sun Casino, where it's my job to monitor disagreements between patrons. That's how I overheard Nori trying to blackmail Lyr."

"What?" Snaps Edith.

That's a serious charge," says Gertie.

"Not to mention one that can't be validated," says Nori. "As we've already established that Lyr Corby is a liar."

"What did you hear Nori say, Lightning?" asks Edith.

"Nori tried to cut a deal with Lyr. She told her she wouldn't tell the Grays about the real parents of her adopted son, if she stepped down and recommended her as the next ombudswoman."

The thunderous hissing that erupts in the room hurts my ears.

"How did Lyr react?" gulps Gertie.

"She refused to cave. She said she wouldn't support Nori for ombudswoman, no matter what."

"Were there any other witnesses?" asks Edith.

"I'm pretty sure a couple of casino regulars heard them arguing," says Lightning.

"Perhaps we should move this line of inquiry into the river," suggests Edith. "Lightning and Nori: do you both agree to let the river determine who is telling the truth?"

"I'm down with that," affirms Lightning.

"No way!" snaps Nori. "I refuse to participate in such superstitious tomfoolery. I revoke my claim to the ombudswoman position."

Gertie pulls out a sprig of cedar from her pocket and places it inside a quahog shell. She lights the cedar and carries the smoking shell around the room, spreading its powerful cleansing smell. The cats in the room snarl. The Grays settle down and offer private blessings. Nori chokes on the smoke.

When Gertie finishes smudging, she returns to her spot beneath the moon and raises her voice, "I now call for a show of hands in support of Snowy Strangeways as our new ombudswoman. This young woman has exhibited incredible courage and dedication to Gray values. She was raised by the famed New York City Ombudswoman, Fríða Olafsdottir, and the late Supreme Gray Goddess Slaney Strangeways. She also saved the lives of three children."

All of the Gray Wolve's hands shoot up, in support of Gertie's recommendation. The Foxes and Goddesses raise their hands more slowly.

Gertie continues, "I also request that the Heralds record the votes of the Silver Sirens on this matter."

Summoner says, "I'll do it, Snowy," and scurries to the dock.

When he returns, he announces that the Sirens have approved me unanimously.

Nori mutters, "Ha! I'm not surprised Snowy got one hundred percent support from a group of women so dangerous that our Gray law won't let them set foot on shore."

"That's enough, Nori," denounces Edith. "The vote is final. We must all respect our new ombudswoman."

Alse, Gertie, Edith, and I join hands in a tight circle under the moon.

"Your installation involves making a covenant with all of the gray groups," whispers Alse.

"A covenant?" I mumble.

Everything spirals before me, as these three older women take turns asking me questions.

Snowy Strangeways:

Do you promise to rule honorably on Gray cases, according to the Rede and Qutuhikan?

I do.

Do you promise to live in Granite House without a child or partner?

I do.

Do you promise to promote justice for all Grays?

I do.

Do you swear these things on Grandmother Moon and the Moon Goddess?

I do.

Do you promise to keep our coven secret?

Say what...

"Semantics," Alse whispers. "'You are making a covenant with our groups. Those groups also need a name. Coven is just one of many names that refers to a secret group of associates. Our ancestral founders chose it because it was used pejoratively against Rebekah. They wanted to take a stand against that injustice."

Gertie's eye twitches. "There's nothing wrong with the word coven, dear."

I raise my eyebrows.

"Allow me to provide some background," offers Alse. "From the 1400s through the 1600s, European men condemned powerful women as witches. Millions were executed. Some of this madness made its way to America. My ancestor, Alse Young, was hung as a witch in Hartford,

Connecticut in 1647. She was merely a woman who knew her own mind. After her death, the women in my family decided to own the name 'coven,' as an act of resistance."

"Fine, but why would Native American women use that name?" I ask.

The three women exchange glances.

Gertie speaks up. "After the English arrived, our Native women ancestors were also forced to lay low, as the colonists were not accustomed to letting their women run the show. Our Native women's groups took meek names like the 'Church Ladies Sewing Society,' in order not to rile the settlers."

"Got it," I say. "But the word coven certainly begs the question: are the Grays witches or wiccan, like everybody claims?" I ask.

Alse shrugs. "Some are. Some aren't," she hedges.

Edith cocks her head. "If you're asking about Gertie and me," she qualifies. "The answer is no. We represent what our Native women have always been. We carry the power of life and healing for our people and the earth. But we also support our Gray sisters from across the sea by claiming and supporting a word that carried the power they were forbidden to use."

"It would appear that I have a lot to learn," I acknowledge. "But as long as you are all in agreement on this, then I promise to protect our secret coven," I pledge.

Gertie slips a charcoal gray judge's robe over my head. It's just the right size but yet-to-be beaded with wampum at the cuffs and collar. I pull my wampum feather necklace out from under my shirt to wear over my robe. Gertie's eyes tear up. Edith places a hand on the wampum feather on my chest.

"This downturned feather is a symbol of peace, Ombudswoman Strangeways," reminds Edith. "We, Grays, are entrusting you with maintaining justice, in order to preserve our very fragile peace. Do you feel up to the task?"

"Not remotely, Supreme Gray Fox," I say. "But I believe in our Gray goals, and I will devote myself to upholding them."

"That's what I hoped to hear." Edith raises her voice, "Fellow Grays, I now present your new ombudswoman, Snowy Strangeways. May she uphold peace and justice in our Gray world for many years to come."

I'm mobbed by hugs, mostly from people I thought hated me.

Lightning approaches, tongue in cheek. "You're hot shit, cousin."

"You think it's time you teach me the old stuff?"

"When you're ready. I agree that you're gonna need all the medicine you can get. But first, I'm thinking you need a serious cleansing ceremony, before your step into the deep shades of gray. You're not gonna refuse it, like your mom, are you?"

"Hell no, Gray sister."

We both put our hands to our hearts, and I swear I feel them beating together.

Gertie waits until everyone else has taken a turn congratulating me, and them pulls me aside. "Ombudswoman, what is your first order of business for the heralds?"

I scan the room. Summoner offers me a shy wave, his eyes filled with concern.

I'm grateful for that wave because it tells me what I need to do. "My first order of business is to offer the heralds a ten percent increase in pay, a path for advancement within our organization, and the option of entering a rehabilitation program for any addictions they may suffer."

The Grays roar with concern. Summoner's jaw drops. The other heralds stare at me, in awe, some clapping cautiously. Edith joins them.

I jump into another topic while I still have momentum. "I have a second order of business."

I pause, to build anticipation.

The room falls silent.

"I wish to end Gray executions."

"Ending executions will change our organizational structure," observes Gertie. "What will this mean for our Lead Executioner, Lara Oakley? And Riley Finch, who serves as the Executioner's Assistant?"

"Lara can retire as the last Gray executioner with a police pension and focus on her fragile health. It's time for a new police chief." I say. "As far as Riley goes, I hereby promote him to Lead Herald."

The heralds clap loudly when they hear this. Riley beams. Barnacle meows.

Edith interjects, "You can do as you wish with the heralds, Snowy. But I need a show of hands on the issue of ending Gray executions."

Less than half the women in the room raise their hands in support.

"Heralds," I call out. "Please record the vote of the Sirens on this issue."

"I told you she was a bad choice." booms Nori, arms smugly folded. "Anything that carries a majority with Siren votes will lead to trouble.

Riley sends Summoner to the Siren's yacht and he returns with two thumbs up. "All of them are on board," he says. "You have a majority."

"I'm glad Riley holds the title of Lead Herald." Edith elbows Nori. "He suffered undue shame in your newspaper for his protection of Amani Jones. He deserves this compensation. *Kutapatush*, Thank you, Snowy."

"I suppose," grumbles Nori.

"Ombudswoman Strangeways." Alse teeters on her infamous cane. "Are there any other earthshattering changes you'd like to make on your first day in office?"

"Yes," I reply. "I'm creating a special herald team to apprehend Gray criminals. It will be led by Summoner, as Summoner-In-Chief."

"Summoner-in-Chief?" Alse flinches.

Summoner tries to stand tall in his frayed gray shirt and ragged gray trousers, covered by a lightweight gray coat with a stain on one sleeve. I catch Alse, Edith, and Gertie grinding their teeth over Summoner's appearance.

"Summoner has been a loyal herald," affirms Edith, lips tight.

"I quite agree," says Gertie."

"I suppose so," grunts Alse, rolling her eyes.

Summoner's video-glazed eyes are the size of Frisbees. His clothing is garbage, his hair is uncombed, and I doubt he's showered. But in one day, he has skyrocketed in pay, position, and prestige.

"How can I be of service, ombudswoman?" he asks me, standing as straight as his rounded gamer's back will allow.

"Summoner-in-Chief, your first assignment is a difficult one. Gather your best men to seek out and summon Zola Black for her violation of the Rede."

CHAPTER 21
COVEN-ANT

Skyscrapers of boxes from my New York home fill my new bedroom on the top floor of Granite House. I chose the room I dubbed Kandinsky's Kiss, now replete with an elliptical yellow bed, a red hexagonal side table, and a blue parallelogram mirror, all designed by me to complement Mom's painting. From way up here, downtown Mystick also looks like a painting. All I can see is an adorable New England village, filled with quaint colonial homes nestled along a gently winding river. I can't see any of the people. This separation can make a person lonely and desperate— like Lyr, or more hideously, like Zola.

I imagine the isolation of those first English colonists in Mystick. There were plenty of Pequots here, when they arrived. Yet, the newcomers never fully saw the humanity of those Natives. Was that due to their sorrow over separation from the people they missed across the sea? Did their desperation to replicate their old society drive them to wipe out those who were here and burn that Pequot village? Could my Mohegan ancestors have stopped them? Were they afraid the same thing would happen to them? Or had the Mohegans grown too close to the English to be objective about them?

I think of Lyr's words. "When you get too close to someone, you lose your objectivity.'"

Lyr and Kai did that with Zola. Manny did that with Mom. But enabling inhumanity is always inexcusable. My job as ombudswoman is to protect our humanity, to guard against the madness that comes with solitude, separation, fear, and loneliness. Sadly, I cannot relieve the loneliness of my new position by hanging out with my Great Aunt Gertie. She stepped down as Supreme Gray Wolf to travel West for some grandmother's gathering to protect a sacred river in the Dakotas. On the bright side, Lightning accepted Gertie's old position as Supreme Gray Wolf, which means I have an ally with whom to shake up this coven.

This COVEN. I still can't get over the name. I told Lightning it sounds risky. She thinks the word is playful and bad ass, like her. She also says it's better than the lame names our tribal women's groups hid behind for the last couple hundred years, like the tribal Church Ladies Sewing Society.

And what is a witch, anyway? A woman who honors the power of the earth? A woman who fights the sort of bad behavior that ran rampant here in 1637?

Naturally, Supreme Gray Fox Edith Wyouggs has decided to stay on, to watch my every move. Considering my problematic pedigree, can you blame her? Yesterday she stopped by to tell me I can't meet Supreme Silver Siren Mab Kincaid, until I've reviewed Lyr's records on the dangerous nature of Sirens. I reassured her that, with a mom like Rebekah and a former partner like Zola, I know quite a bit about handling dangerous women. But Edith disagreed. She checked in again, this morning, to see if I had gotten around to reading those Siren records and was disappointed to find me chatting with Armando, after he dropped off my boxes from The City. As soon as he left, I spread the Siren records across the top of my beautiful new dining table, created by Zura and Ivor. The money I earned from selling Mermaid Cottage and Slaney's business to Brook Beemer paid for that table and the rest of my planned renovation work at Granite House. Brook's extensive Gray training coupled with the newfound silver in her hair won her Slaney's old position of Supreme Gray Goddess. The Grays have been lining up to view the amazing sea glass sign she created for her new business, "Mermaid Cottage Designs." Slaney would be proud.

I enter the kitchen that Fríða has begun to renovate, and pour myself a now-familiar cup of seaweed tea. I grab a granny smith apple from the fireplace cauldron I originally commissioned from the Mystick Seaport blacksmith for Monster House. Over that fireplace, Alse has promised to paint me a (not-too-colorful) mural of Goddess Cerridwen of the Cauldron, keeper of wisdom.

I return to the dining room and settle into reviewing the Siren papers. My harsh brass doorbell clangs, signaling the arrival of a visitor. I'm ready for Edith, this time, and rush to the stone foyer. I'm even wearing a wampum-colored leather summer shorts suit, purchased at her tribe's Foxwoods Casino. I shove open the heavy rock door. But it's not Edith who stands before me.

"Dad," I gasp.

Manny is no longer the wild-eyed giant in a long gray gabardine duster with monstrous pewter boots. He's sporting a distressed gray jacket, gray jeans, running shoes, and a faded gray baseball cap that make him look, well, almost like a Mystick local.

"Before you say anything. Need to know some things." He inhales. "Never wanted to leave you. Grays fired me. Kicked me out of the country. Had to take lousy jobs where I could get them. Lyr reinstated me after Slaney died."

I fold my arms. "I remember Lyr arguing with Fríða at Slaney's funeral. They must have been fighting over you. Fríða probably didn't think you should be allowed to return because you aren't trustworthy. She's right. I get why you didn't visit me while you were banished. But you didn't have to ditch me after Zola's open house. You could have admitted you were my dad when we first met. But you made me figure it out on my own. You knew Riley was the herald who helped Lara execute Rebekah. But you misled me about him. You knew Clancy had nothing to do with Mom's death. Yet you ragged on him because of his affair with Mom."

"I'm only human." Manny slifts the heavy silver, wampum, and pearl pendant hanging from my neck. "What's this?"

I lift up the necklace. "Lyr left this to me, with a note that said, 'wishing you the protection of sea and silver.' I know how you must feel about this necklace, knowing that the woman who gave it to me sentenced Mom to death. But I don't disagree with Lyr's judgement on that case.

By the way, why'd Lyr reinstate you, anyway?"

He shrugs. "She wanted to make sure you had a family."

"I have a whole tribe. And I have the Grays."

"Wasn't sure the Mohegans would accept you. Your Great Uncle Lake hated me and your mom."

"He hates everybody."

"Wait a minute, when did Lyr reinstate you?"

"After Slaney died."

I turn the full force of my infamous crow black eyes on Dad. "When were you going to tell me the truth about who you are?"

He slumps. "Wanted to, right along. Was afraid you'd reject me."

I put a hand on my hip. "Next time, take a chance on the truth. You've spent too much time lying to people, in your glamorous career as a globe-trotting detective."

"Not so glamorous. Spend a lot of time alone."

"Be careful about being alone, too much. There's no need for it. You have family now."

He searches my face. "Sure. But it doesn't look like you forgive me."

"Family isn't always friendly," I advise. "Why did you vanish after the open house for Mystick Picnick?"

"Panic. Was already suspicious of Zola. Wasn't sure why. Once I realized she was Zena, I came back. Same day, you found the kidnapped kids. Kai sprung her. What a mess. Brought back bad memories. Your mom didn't murder Lucy Wauby, by the way. Zena, Zola—or whatever she calls herself— she did it."

I push his huge chest away. "By the Goddess, Dad! I'll bet Kai thinks it was the other way around. I'm sure he believes that Rebekah was the one who made his mom go bad."

He points two stickup fingers at me. "Zola messed with that kid's head."

I point two stickup fingers right back at him. "News flash, Dad. Mom did the same thing to you. Both women belonged behind bars but manipulated men to help them escape. Rebekah and Zola are murderers. You and Kai helped them, out of love, not because they were innocent."

He tries to set his jaw. "Won't ever think badly of Rebekah." He opens his arms. "Can I get a hug from my daughter?"

I expect to resist but find myself falling into his arms. "Followed your work in The City," he whispers in my ear. "Snuck into the country for every show you had at Víðsýni."

"No way," I snivel.

He pulls back and crosses his heart. "Had to be super-discreet. Hats, dark sunglasses, the whole friggin' bit. Fríða never got over me getting your mom pregnant at sixteen."

I break into a laugh, letting go. "I can't hold that against you. It's the only reason I'm here. Plus, I'm old enough to understand how that sort of thing happens, Dad. I'm not a kid anymore."

"True. But you've had it rough, even for a grown woman. Hear your boyfriend's AWOL."

I raise a hand. "Hold up! Kai's not my boyfriend. Even if he were here, he'd probably be hooking up with his ex, the lovely Supreme Gray Goddess Brook Beemer, newly of Mermaid Cottage. There's no future for us. I'm forced to lead a hermit's life as ombudswoman, remember?"

He snorts. "Think these Grays follow their rules?"

I mimic his snort. "Mom sure didn't. I got this job because Lyr didn't. But I've only been ombudswoman for less than a week. I hope to get through my first month without a major violation." I wag an accusing finger at him. "Besides, the last thing you should be doing is encouraging another Gray woman to break the rules. Your track record sucks."

"True enough." He examines his shuffling feet. "You worried Zola might hurt more kids?"

"Yup."

"Me, too."

Manny's phone rings. He excuses himself and steps aside. An incredulous look falls over his face, as he hangs up.

"That was Kai Corby," he huffs.

"What?" I ask with more enthusiasm than I would like. "Where is he? Wait...why did he call you?"

"I asked him to phone, if he ever knew anything. Turns out he does. Your heralds just caught up to him."

"I knew that Summoner would come through," I revel.

"Sure did. Summoner told him you were the new ombudswoman, that you did right by the Heralds. Kai led him straight to Zola. Said he's sick of her crazy. Took him a week to figure out she was nuts. Took her less to figure she didn't want a son."

"Ouch," I say, biting my tongue. There's no point in telling Manny that I know how Kai feels because my mom didn't want me, either. He loved Rebekah too much to see her faults.

"Is Kai in custody?" I ask.

"Lara let him go, due to his cooperation," explains Manny.

"Where's Zola?" I ask.

"Heralds are guarding her on a boat on the river."

"Like a Siren?"

"Will be, soon enough. Can't kill her."

"Because of my stupid new rule?"

"No, because you've only got her on *attempted* murder."

I grimace. "I don't like the idea of Zola hanging out on a yacht on the river that's filled with wicked women. It feels like we're brewing a storm on our own shore." My mind drifts back to the subject of Kai. "I wonder why Kai contacted you and not me."

"Said he phoned Mermaid Cottage. Nobody answered. Didn't tell him you'd moved out. Or that Brook was moving in."

"Much obliged, Dad."

Manny peers up at the ceiling, "Hold your thanks. He's on his way here."

I tug at my purple jacket. "What! Kai's coming here? He can't live here anymore!"

"Technically, he can. Was legal before. But you'd be the judge of such things, now, Ombudswoman."

"Don't you think I should prohibit it?"

"Ombudswomen's lives are lonely. You said it yourself."

"A herald's life isn't much better, from what I've seen."

"Which is why I keep busy. Give me an assignment. Then you can start worrying about Kai showing up." He bows, "Put me to work."

I try to remember that Manny is one of my heralds, and not just my long-lost dad. "Grayshield, I believe you've learned from your mistakes. Therefore, I hereby name you Chief Herald Investigator."

"Chief Herald Investigator. Sounds great. Sounds like I should have staff."

"Don't push it." I say. "I already busted the Gray's budget by increasing the herald's salaries and offering benefits."

"Fair enough." He points to the weapons' case in the room behind me. "What you doin' with those weapons, when there's no more executions?"

"I'm maintaining them as the dismal souvenirs of a bygone era."

"An era I'd rather forget," gulps Manny.

"Not everything about Mystick's past is dark, Dad. Come upstairs. Let me show you something."

We link arms. I lead him into the second-floor bedroom next door to mine. "Check it out," I point to the mural on the wall. "Lyr never showed me this room. I only discovered it after I moved in."

Manny gawps. "Isn't this the mural from the basement where the cops found Lucy's body? What's it doing here?"

"Bingo. I wondered the same thing. So, I contacted Lyr, in Brazil, and asked her. She said Lucy was not killed in that abandoned house. Rebekah put her body there because she knew the place was up for demolition. She figured the dynamite would take care of hiding her crime. Then I showed up, before she covered up her handiwork. The house was owned by the same Pequot woman who painted the mural. She painted her name in one corner. It says "Dancing Fox." When I discovered it, I was awestruck. There's a lesson in this mural, endless lessons in fact."

He examines the artwork. "The river is clean and full of life. None of that gaudy tropical bullshit that Alse paints. No weird symbolism, like your mom's art. No boring colors, like Slaney's work." He rubs his chin, "Simple, straight up, bright, and true. My kind of art."

I offer a weak smile. "Not as simple as you might think. Notice the swirling lines and shadows? What you're seeing are the shades of gray; the ever circling, interconnected, spiraling, natural world. This shows the workings of Mystick when it was an indigenous village, four hundred years ago, back when the Mohegans and Pequots were one tribe, before the English came. It's an image of a time when the hills were covered with cornfields; the rivers jumped with sturgeon, the skies teamed with eagles, and the spirits of the four winds guided people's lives. Our brothers and sisters didn't just walk on two feet: they also wore fins, feathers, and bounded on all fours."

"Trippy. Do you meditate in here?" asks Manny with a snicker.

"Funny. I come here to remember why my job as ombudswoman

matters."

"Wait a minute? What's that sound?" Manny perks up. "I thought I heard something mewing? But I know you hate cats."

"Correction. That was before I became Gray Ombudswoman. I took Zola's cat in after the heralds rescued him from behind the walls of Monster House."

"Never thought of you as the nurturing type."

"I never had to save the lives of three kids and a kitten, before." I touch the river whitecaps, painted on the mural. "Some days, I don't need this mural to recall Mystick's past; I gaze outside and my visions turn back the clock. I see people fishing in dugout canoes. I fast forward to the first colonial houses and tall sailing ships that appeared on these shores. An instant later, I'm back to the present. Occasionally, I even glimpse the future."

"Lyr had visions, too. Must be some kind of job qualification for Ombudswomen," he observes.

I take Manny's hand. "I also have serious dreams. Last night, I dreamt that the white colonial houses along the river were pealing, right down to their bare wood clapboards. The clapboards were charred black, underneath, like those seventeenth century Pequot wigwams. The townspeople tried to cover those burned clapboards with coat after coat of white paint. But that burned wood couldn't be concealed by all the white paint in the world."

He squeezes my hand. "How you gonna fix that, Snowy?"

I answer, as his ombudswoman. "That's the hard work of the Grays. Isn't it? That's what Edith, Brook, Lightning, and I are tasked to do. Healing this town is an ongoing process. A river runs through it, forever cleansing, washing our crimes back out into the Great Salt Sea. We also enjoy the guiding white light of the moon that forever shows us the path out of darkness, towards peace and justice."

"Amen, ombudswoman." He tosses both thumbs at his chest. "Now. . . about my job."

I blink. "Seriously? We talk for the first time in my life, and you act like I'm the Gray's Human Resources Manager?"

He shrugs in a Brooklyn kind of way. "Live to work. Work to live. A herald's duty. Yada, yada."

I close my eyes and remind myself that I've been confiding in a man who hardly knows me, a man who is also my employee. "Fine. Grayshield, your first assignment is to find out what happened to my grandfather, Wolfie."

"That guy? Could be dead, or anywhere."

"Good thing you're such a great globetrotting investigator. Your first clue about his whereabouts is a letter I found, blackmailing Zola into giving up her New York business. It's signed "W." If that "W" stands for "Wolfie," he could be close by, watching and waiting. I don't want him to die of old age without me trying to reach out to him."

"Lemme see it."

I hand him a copy of the letter.

Manny shuffles. "W for Wolfie? It's possible. Seems he had it out for Zola. Wonder if he found out that banishing her from The City drove her back to Mystick. Just so you know, this Wolfie guy is not my biggest fan. And it's mutual."

"That's because you both loved Rebekah. We all have trouble being objective about the people and places we love. Take how tourists view Mystick. They love this adorable historic New England town, with its seaport, drawbridge, cider mill, and white colonial homes along a picaresque river. They don't consider the many millennia of events and history the preceded the era of that colonial architecture. More important, they'll never know that it's taken centuries of hardscrabble cooperation between those who've lived here since the colonial era and those who greeted their boats to maintain peace and justice in Mystick."

He starts clapping. "You sound like Gertie. Which is a good thing. Never had a problem with that woman. Maybe she's got a lead on Wolfie."

Manny kisses me on the cheek. "Time to get to work," he says, all business.

I give him a thumbs up.

He pops those two index fingers at me and walks out the door.

The minute I close it, I feel empty.

Why didn't I wish him luck?

Why didn't I kiss him back?

Why didn't I act like a daughter, instead of a boss?

Why didn't I try harder to act more like a daughter and less like I throw the door back open, intent on catching him and sharing a better goodbye. But a different man stands before me. He has driftwood curls, skin like a wet beach, a scar across his nose, and a permanent notch in his finger from overusing his stupid copper pen. He's wearing a torn rumpled shirt and an abandoned puppy look.

I lean back, toss a hand on my hip and say, "Look what the heralds dragged in."

Kai leans in. "Have you rented my room, yet?"

I raise an eyebrow. "Your annex is not part of Granite House. You're free to stay, unless you give me some reason to evict you."

"Good to know." His eyes narrow at the sight of the silver, pearl, and wampum medallion I'm wearing. "That's..." he swallows.

"A gift from your mother . . . I mean Lyr."

"Lyr is my only mom."

"So you're a good guy, again?"

"Well, yeah. The necklace suits you, by the way." He moves toward me.

I back up. "Kai, I need to be careful because the women in my family have lousy judgement when it comes to men."

"Our dads also had lousy taste in women." He pauses a moment. "Zola played me, like she played everyone else. It was stupid of me to fall for her brokenhearted mom routine."

"I hear you. I believed the best of my murderous mom, as well."

He moves in, again. "If you're not in the midst of another business event, we can swap bad mom jokes all day. Or, you could invite me in," he smirks.

I grab Kai's oxford collar and pull him into the cool stone entryway. I press my mouth onto his. We become the river, again. Soft and rough, and rocky and wild. Everything that ever was or will be resides in that kiss.

"The river," I sigh.

"Sorry?" says Kai.

"We're like the river, forever flowing, like time with occasional ripples of dark tides."

He breaks away. "About those dark tides, I should probably tell you that I'm unemployed. I'm wondering if maybe we can just be like everybody else our age—trying to find mediocre jobs, scraping by, floundering our way through the world."

I tug on one of his springy curls. "Or, we can do it my way." I adjust my suit jacket. "I'm an eighteen-year-old design prodigy, living in a well-appointed stone mansion, hired to preside over a four-hundred-year-old organization, managed by several secret women's groups, composed of goddesses, wolves, foxes, and sirens, and manned by my own personal army of heralds."

"Or that." he shrugs, squinting one eye. "I have some skills that might prove useful. I know most of the rare plants and animals on this hill. Maybe I could be your forest warden. Some of these trees are older than this town. They're among the wisest members of our Mystick community." He offers me his arm. "May I introduce you to them."

"I would like that, my Perhaps Friend," I smile.

He runs a finger across my lips, glossed in cedar red. "Or perhaps more?"

THE END

About the Author

Melissa Tantaquidgeon Zobel is anenrolled member of the Mohegan Tribe of Connecticut. She grew up giving tours at Tantaquidgeon Museum, run by her great-aunt and great uncle, Medicine Woman Gladys Tantaquidgeon and Chief Harold Tantaquidgeon. Those elders trained her in tribal oral tradition, traditional lifeways, and spiritual beliefs. She earned a B.S.F.S. in history/diplomacy from Georgetown University, an M.A. in history from the University of Connecticut, and an M.F.A. in creative writing from Fairfield University. As a young adult, she worked as Mohegan Federal Recognition Coordinator, researching and organizing her tribe's successful bid for federal acknowledgment. She was appointed tribal historian in 1991 and Medicine Woman in 2008. Her awards include an Emmy for the movie, *The Mark of Uncas*, the Native Writers of the Americas First Book Award, the Alaskan Federation of Natives' National Essay Award, and Tomaquag Museum's Native American Scholar Award. Zobel's previous books include *Medicine Trail: The Life and Lessons of Gladys Tantaquidgeon* (University of Arizona Press, 2000), *Oracles*, (University of New Mexico Press, 2004), and *Wabanaki Blues* (Poisoned Pen Press, 2015). She is married to her high school sweetheart Randy Zobel and lives in Mystic, Connecticut.

CPSIA information can be obtained
at www.ICGtesting.com
Printed in the USA
BVHW03s2331290318
511990BV00001B/1/P

9 781988 214191